BOYS ROCK!

■ ■ ■ ■ ■ ■

BOYS ROCK!

Phyllis Reynolds Naylor

SCHOLASTIC INC.
New York Toronto London Auckland Sydney
Mexico City New Delhi Hong Kong Buenos Aires

ISBN-13: 978-0-545-04249-9
ISBN-10: 0-545-04249-6

12 11 10 9 8 7 6 5 4 3 2 1   8 9 10 11 12/0

Printed in the U.S.A.   40

First Scholastic printing, January 2008

The text of this book is set in 12-point Adobe Garamond.

*To Michael Oldaker
and his bookstore*

Contents

■   ■   ■   ■   ■   ■

BOYS ROCK!

■ ■ ■ ■ ■ ■

■ ■ ■ ■ ■ ■ ■ ■ ■ ■ ■

One

■

Starting Now

It was the day after the Fourth of July. The sun was warm, the air was breezy, and time was moving slowly, just the way Wally liked it. No clock telling him to get up, no bell ringing for class—just twelve hours stretching out before him, with only a wisp of leftover firework smoke in his nostrils.

But Wally Hatford had come to a decision. Since he was ninety-nine percent sure that the Malloy girls would be moving back to Ohio when summer was over, he didn't want any guilt feelings hanging around once they were gone. So he was going to be super-nice to them.

Well, maybe not *super*-nice. Maybe not even nice, exactly. But he would probably be polite. Okay, maybe not *polite* polite, but he certainly wasn't going to do anything to make them mad. Especially Caroline.

Wally had just finished reading the first book on his

summer reading list, *A Ghost's Revenge,* and it was one of the creepiest, scariest stories he had ever read.

The book said that each person has a ghostly self that shadows him all the time, whether he knows it or not. When the person dies, the ghost takes over, but even when the person is alive, that ghostly self can make its presence known if it gets mad enough. Sometimes it even latches on to that person's enemy and haunts *him* for a while. *Forever,* even!

In the story, a man cheated his neighbor, and after a time the neighbor moved away, but the neighbor's ghost didn't. It hung around to get even. Everything the man tried to do went wrong. His vegetables wouldn't grow, his car broke down, his dog got sick, and his roof caught fire.

This worried Wally a lot.

It was only a story, of course. Wally *knew* that. But if the Malloy girls moved back to Ohio, where they used to live, Wally did not want their ghostly selves, if they had any, hanging around *him.* If they moved away, he did not want one of those ghostly selves—especially Caroline's—trying to settle a score with the boy who maybe hadn't treated her as well as he could have. It was only a piece of nonsense, but it didn't stop Wally from dreaming that he heard a *scritch, scratch, scritch* in the cellar. Then a soft *thump, thumpity, thump* on the stairs. Then a *creak, crickety, creak* of the floorboards in his bedroom, and then an icy hand. . . .

"Yipe!" Wally said aloud, suddenly snapping to attention as his twin brothers came out on the porch.

"What's the matter with you? Got ants in your pants?" said Jake as he flopped down on the glider and Josh took a wicker chair. Wally had been sitting on the floor, leaning against a post.

"Something like that," said Wally, giving his head a shake.

If Mom and Dad knew all the tricks he and his brothers had played on those Malloy girls, Wally thought . . . ! Of course, the girls had played their share of pranks too, but the truth was, the boys had started it. And though Wally had usually gone along reluctantly, he had definitely been involved. He had most certainly done things he shouldn't have. A ghostly presence would remember that. Wally didn't care if their vegetables didn't grow, but he didn't want their car to break down or their roof to catch fire, just because he hadn't been nicer to Caroline Malloy.

Jake stretched his long legs out in front of him and pulled a sheet of paper from his jeans pocket. After unfolding it section by section, he pointed to the print at the top of the page. "Listen, Wally," he said. "You want to be in on something? If Josh and I put out a neighborhood newspaper, that counts as three books on our summer reading list. You want to help out?"

By now, Wally had learned that whenever Jake had an idea, alarm bells should go off right, left, and every which way from Sunday. Still, a newspaper might be fun. . . .

"Just any kind of newspaper?" he asked.

"It has to be three issues of a newspaper about

historical stuff in Buckman. That shouldn't be too hard," Jake answered.

It did sound sort of interesting. "So what would *I* get to be?" asked Wally. "Manager? Photographer? What?"

"We thought maybe you could be the spell checker. You know . . . go over the stuff we write," Josh explained.

"Forget it," said Wally, and settled back against the post again. If there was a least attractive job to do, it was always Wally who got to do it.

Jake pulled a Three Musketeers bar out of his pocket and held it out toward Wally. "You'd be good at it," he said.

Wally knew he was a good speller. Whenever he came across a new word, it lit up in his brain like a neon sign. But he didn't like the idea of Jake and Josh having all the fun; he wanted to be something more than spell checker.

"No deal," he said.

"We'll have a great time," said Josh.

"So, have a blast," Wally told him.

Jake held the candy bar a little closer. "Okay, you can be spell checker *and* distributor. How about that?"

"What does the distributor do?" asked Wally.

"Sees that the newspaper gets around," said Jake.

"You mean, take it door to door," said Wally.

"Well, that, too," said Jake. The candy bar came closer still. Wally guessed it was an old one left over from last Halloween. Tucked away in a sock drawer, maybe.

"You'd also get your name on the masthead along with ours," said Josh.

That was more like it. Wally reached for the candy bar, unwrapped it, and took a bite. It *tasted* like old socks too!

"The only problem," said Josh, "is that even with you and Peter helping out, it's still going to be a lot of work. We're wondering if maybe we should ask the Malloys to go in on it with us."

Wally closed his eyes. Hadn't they gotten in enough trouble with Eddie, Beth, and Caroline over the past year? Why did they have to go *looking* for disaster? "Are you nuts?" he asked.

"It's just a thought," said Jake.

"If they move back to Ohio, Eddie won't get summer reading credit for putting out a newspaper. Why would she want to help? Why would Beth and Caroline want to be in on it at all? They're not even in the same grade as you," Wally said.

Jake and Josh had been in sixth grade along with Eddie Malloy, Beth had been in fifth, and Wally had been stuck down in fourth grade with Caroline. The last thing in the world Wally wanted to do was to spend a summer around her.

"Maybe they'd just like to do it for fun. It's one way to spend July," said Josh.

"As if they couldn't find stuff to do on their own," said Wally. "If they get to be on our newspaper, Eddie will try to be boss and you know it."

"I've already thought of that," Jake told him. "So I've named myself editor. I'm going to write up stories, and Josh will draw some comics. We'll tell the girls they can choose any job they want on the newspaper except editor, illustrator, or distributor."

Well, maybe that wouldn't be too bad, Wally thought. No reason the girls couldn't do their part on their side of the river, and the Hatfords could do their work over here. If anyone crossed the swinging footbridge that they used to go back and forth, it wouldn't have to be often and it wouldn't have to be Wally.

He looked across the river at the white house on Island Avenue. The Malloys were renting it from the Bensons, the best friends the Hatford brothers had ever had. The Buckman River flowed into town on one side of Island Avenue, circled around under the road bridge leading to the business district, and flowed out again on the other side.

"Man oh man, if the Bensons were back, we could sure put out a good newspaper," Wally said. "We could have a production line going you wouldn't believe."

"Yeah, well, they're not back, because Steve and Tony signed up for a bunch of summer stuff down there, and so did Bill and Danny and Doug," said Josh disgustedly.

"We figured they'd be back here the second that school let out in Georgia. We figured wrong," said Jake.

Wally could hear seven-year-old Peter come banging in the back door. The screen door slammed, the refrig-

6

erator door thumped, and there were footsteps coming down the hall; then the front screen door flew open. Peter was trailing sand from the sandbox Mrs. Hatford had brought home from the hardware store.

Sucking on an orange Popsicle, he sat down on the glider beside Jake. Because both Mr. and Mrs. Hatford worked during the day, Peter's three older brothers were responsible for him until their parents came home.

"What's everyone doing?" Peter asked.

"Planning a newspaper," said Jake. "Want to help?"

"Will I get my name in it?" Peter asked.

"Absolutely," said Jake. "On the very first page."

Well, if even Peter was going to be in on it, Wally decided, he would be too. This was probably one of the last things the Hatfords and the Malloys would do together. If he was going to be nice, it had better be now. If he was going to be polite, that meant starting today. If he was just going to get along, well . . . he could do that, too.

■ ■ ■ ■ ■ ■ ■ ■ ■ ■ ■

Two

■

Call from Jake

Caroline perched in her father's big chair and didn't move a muscle. Her eyes were closed, her hands folded, and she sat very straight, shoulders not even touching the back of the chair. Her long brown ponytail came almost to her waist, but it didn't move either. Not a fraction of an inch. She looked like a sculpture in an art museum.

When twelve-year-old Eddie walked into the room, apple in hand, Caroline said softly, "Eddie, did you sense anything just now?"

Eddie stopped chewing. "Huh?"

"Before you came into the room, did you sense that I was here? Do I have an aura or anything?"

"An *aroma*, you mean? Are you asking if you smell?"

"No, I was reading a book about famous actresses, and it said that some of them—like Greta Garbo—had a certain aura about them. People could tell almost before they entered a room that she was in it, or that she had just left."

"Probably her perfume," said Eddie.

Caroline, who longed to be in the movies herself or to be an actress on Broadway, shook her head. "A good actress sends out vibrations," she said.

"Well, don't send any vibrations my way, Caroline," her sister told her, plunking herself down on the couch. "I want a peaceful summer."

Caroline sighed. It was hard being precocious. It was difficult enough to have skipped a grade and to have to go through school with kids a year older than you— Wally Hatford, to be precise—but even worse when your own family couldn't understand what you were talking about.

She concentrated again on producing an aura. She imagined every cell on her scalp tingling at the approach of another person, every hair on her head giving off electricity. Perhaps if she hummed very softly—one long, low note—it would help people sense her aura before they ever entered the room.

"*Hmmmmm,*" she hummed.

Beth, the middle sister, came into the living room just then. Not only did she not hear Caroline's hum, she didn't see Caroline's feet and stumbled over them as she crossed the rug. Of course, Beth tripped a lot because she always had her nose stuck in a book. She and Eddie were as blond as Caroline was dark, and the two older girls often joked that Caroline must have been found along the side of the road, because she didn't resemble anyone else in the family.

"I don't know why you're bothering with your summer reading list," Eddie said, looking at Beth. "I'm not bothering with mine because we probably won't even be here in September."

"But if Dad decides we'll stay in Buckman, you'll be in big trouble, Eddie," Beth told her.

Eddie only shrugged. "We'll know by August. If we stay, I'll catch up on my reading then. Besides, the seventh graders here get credit for three books if they produce three newspapers on Buckman's history. I'd rather do the newspaper."

Caroline stopped humming and turned around in the armchair. "So why don't you, Eddie, whether we go or stay? I'd like to help write a newspaper. That might be fun!"

Beth lowered the mystery book she was reading, *Cave of the Spider Women.* "Yeah, let's do it, Eddie! I could write an article on the haunted houses of Buckman," she offered.

"*What* houses?" asked Eddie.

"I don't know, but there have to be some! Buckman's an old town, and all old towns have ghosts. Besides, if a newspaper's not interesting, no one will read it. And that would make it interesting!"

Eddie wiggled one foot while she thought it over. Finally she began to smile. "Oh, what the heck, let's do it. Let's start a newspaper."

Caroline clapped her hands.

"I get to be editor, of course," Eddie added.

"Of course," said Beth.

"Then what would *I* do?" asked Caroline. "Something interesting, Eddie."

"Janitor?" Eddie teased.

"Something important!" Caroline demanded.

"I suppose you could write obituaries," said Eddie.

"What's that?"

"Little stories about people who have died," said Beth.

"All right!" said Caroline. "Could I be like a reporter? Go around interviewing their relatives and everything?"

"Sure, if you can find any," said Eddie. "Knock yourself out. But these have to be historical people, you know. They can't just have died yesterday."

At that very moment the phone rang, and Caroline went into the hall to answer.

"Hey!" came Jake's voice. "Could I talk to Eddie or somebody?"

"*I'm* somebody!" said Caroline.

"I mean somebody normal," said Jake. "Let me talk to Eddie."

Caroline held out the phone. "Phone call for a normal person!" she called. "Eddie, it's for you."

Eddie swung her legs off the couch and ambled over.

"It's Jake," Caroline whispered to Beth, who had followed them out into the hall.

Eddie held the phone away from her ear as the girls always did when they talked to a Hatford. They wanted the others to hear.

"Hi," Eddie said. "What's up?"

11

"Josh and I were looking at our summer reading list, and we've decided to do the newspaper. We wondered if you guys were interested," Jake told her. "You know, go in on it with us."

"Why would we be interested when we might be moving back to Ohio?" said Eddie, winking at Beth and Caroline.

"It would be something to do," said Jake.

"Who would do what?" asked Eddie.

"Josh says he'll draw a cartoon and Wally's going to be distributor and take the papers around," Jake said.

"That figures," said Eddie. "What about you?"

"Editor, of course," said Jake.

"Yeah?" said Eddie. "Who elected *you* editor?"

"Well, *some*body's got to be in charge. What would you like to do for the paper?"

"I don't know," said Eddie. "Beth and Caroline might go along with it, but I'm not sure I want to be a part of this."

"Why not?" said Jake.

"Because all the good jobs are taken."

"No way," said Jake. "There are plenty of things you could do."

"If you get to be editor, then can I choose something else? Any job at all?" Eddie asked.

"Sure!" said Jake.

"Positive?"

"Yeah! Just name it. What do you want to be?" Jake asked.

"Editor in chief," said Eddie.

Three

■

Under the Floorboards

There was a cloudburst just after dinner, and Wally went back out onto the porch to watch. He loved being on the porch during a hard rain, water cascading out the downspouts, the air thick with a damp-earth smell.

He liked to figure things out, and once the rain had stopped, he wanted to watch water drip through a crack in the gutter overhead. As less and less water ran down the shingles and into the gutters, the drips came farther and farther apart. Wally was counting the seconds between drops. "One . . . two . . . . three . . . . . four . . . . . . five . . . ."

Out came Jake and Josh and Peter. Just once in his life, Wally thought, he would like to enjoy a rain or an anthill or a spiderweb without interruption. He would like to count drops or drips or ants or all the separate sections of a spiderweb without one of his three brothers barging in to ask, "What are you *doing,* Wally?"

Wally was on the porch floor, actually, lying on his back, trying to see exactly where in the gutter the drops were leaking out.

"Counting," said Wally, and got up, crawling over to the steps again. No one ever understood when he tried to explain things to them, so he wasn't going to try.

"Well, we've got problems," said Jake. "Eddie's going to be editor in chief, so she gets to run the whole show."

Wally looked up, surprised. "How did *that* happen?"

"She's tricky, that's what! But here's our ace in the hole, here's what hotshot Eddie never thought about: if she asks any one of us to do something we don't like—something really awful—it's all for one and one for all. We're in this together, and we strike. If the workers on a newspaper go on strike, it means no newspaper, unless the editor in chief does it all herself."

"What if she doesn't care?" said Wally. "What if she figures she won't even *be* here when September comes and you have to turn in your summer reading reports?"

"She'll care," Josh put in, "because I'm going to make posters and put them all over town announcing the newspaper. *The Hatford Herald,* the signs will read. *Coming July Sixteenth! Eddie Malloy, Editor in Chief.*"

"The *Hatford Herald*?" asked Wally in amazement. "Did Eddie agree to that?"

"Nope," said Jake. "She doesn't even know. But by the time the posters are up all over Buckman, with her on the masthead, she'll have to go along with it. If she tells people she never agreed to the name, it will look as though she's not in charge. And Eddie could never stand for that."

"Anyway," said Josh, "as the new distributor, would you go down to the bookstore and ask Mr. Oldaker if we can leave a pile of newspapers in his store each week for people to pick up? You know . . . explain the whole thing to him. Turn on the *charm,* Wally."

One . . . two . . . . three . . . . . four . . . . . . five . . . . six . . . . seven . . . . The water drops were really slowing down now. Wally wanted to see how long it would take after the rain had quit for the water in the gutter to stop dripping altogether. This always happened. If there was something fun to do, he didn't get to do it. But if there was work or a walk or a mess or a fuss to deal with, guess who got stuck?

He didn't have any charm, and the bookstore probably didn't have any room for stacks of homemade newspapers that kids brought in. What if twenty other kids who were entering seventh grade decided to make one? That was why someone had to go talk to Mike Oldaker in person. That was why someone had to turn on the charm. That was why Wally had to give up an interesting evening on the porch to try out some charm he didn't have on a bookstore owner who didn't have any space.

He thought of telling the twins that he'd changed his mind. He didn't want to be part of this newspaper after all. But if his brothers were busy for the rest of the month looking up words in the dictionary and writing stories, guess who Dad would choose to clean out the shed? If Jake and Josh were going back and forth to the library to find historical stuff, guess who Mom would pick to mow the grass? Why wasn't counting drips from a rain gutter as important as drawing a comic strip? Wally wanted to know.

"All right," he said, his voice flat. "I'll go."

While Jake and Josh and Peter went upstairs to play computer games, Wally went down the steps and started toward the business district. The Buckman River, to his left, seemed to have no more energy than Wally did. Despite the earlier rain, it flowed so slowly that it appeared hardly to be moving at all. Everything seemed to have come to a standstill this summer, one of the hottest on record.

Lights shone now along College Avenue, however, and more people were out and about now that the air was a little cooler. Some of the shops stayed open till seven or eight or nine o'clock, and as Wally turned onto Main Street, he was sort of glad he had come. At least he could look over the comic books while he was in the bookstore.

When he came to Oldakers', he had to walk up one row of books and down another before he found Mike Oldaker, the owner, who was unloading a box of mystery books and putting them on a shelf.

"Looking for anything in particular, Wally?" Mike asked.

"Just you," said Wally. "You see, we're sort of . . . uh . . . putting out a newspaper. . . ."

"Let me guess," said Mike. "Jake and Josh are doing it as part of the seventh-grade summer reading project, right? And you got roped into helping out."

Wally stared in amazement. "Right. How did you know?"

"Because seventh graders get a project like this every year, and they always want to know if I'll keep a stack of their newspapers in my store."

Wally gulped. "So . . . uh . . ."

Mike smiled. "And every year it's the same. It sounds like a good idea at the beginning, but when kids find out how much work's involved, usually only two or three end up doing it. So what's the name of your paper—have you thought of one yet?"

"The *Hatford Herald*," said Wally.

"Okay. You've got yourself a deal. If you guys actually manage to print the first issue, and you do a good job, I'll make space for you on the shelf by the window."

Wally could scarcely believe his good luck. Did this mean he wouldn't have to walk all over Buckman knocking on doors? That he wouldn't have to stand on the corner by the courthouse yelling, "The *Hatford Herald*! Come and get it! *Hatford Herald*! Absolutely free!"

At that very moment Wally thought he heard a noise coming from under the floorboards. He glanced toward the trapdoor in the hardwood floor of the old bookstore, the trapdoor that led to the cellar, where the boys had once trapped Caroline. It was closed. There was no sign of any workmen.

Wally looked at Mike Oldaker, but the owner had gone back to unpacking books, picking them up two at a time and shoving them onto a shelf. There was another sound, sort of a slow, scraping sound, like someone clawing at the bare earth floor of that cellar.

Wally turned to see if any other customers had noticed, but no one else seemed to have heard. Maybe he'd only imagined it, because Mike Oldaker didn't let anyone go down there, where there was only dirt and dust and mice and cobwebs.

But then . . . there it was again. *Scraping, scraping . . . clawing, clawing.* Very strange. "Mike?" Wally said.

This time Mike stopped shelving books. This time he, too, took a quick look around, as though to see if any other customers were listening. Then he came back over to Wally, one finger to his lips.

"You heard it too, didn't you?" he said.

Wally nodded. "What is it?"

"Can you keep a secret?" Mike asked.

Wally nodded again, even though he wasn't sure. What was he supposed to say? That no, he couldn't keep a secret?

"You can't tell anyone, not even your brothers," said Mike. "When it's time, I'll let you know what you're hearing down there, and your newspaper can have the story."

"But we're only doing three issues!" Wally said. "The third one comes out the last week of July. Will you tell me before then?"

"I hope so," said Mike, looking mysterious.

"Can't you at least tell me what's down there? We won't print anything till you say so," Wally said.

Mike Oldaker leaned closer. "Bones," he whispered.

Wally's back stiffened. *Oh,* no! He wasn't going to fall for that! Last November, when a cougar had appeared around Buckman from time to time, but no one saw it long enough to be able to tell what it was, the newspaper had jokingly called it an abaguchie. And the Hatford boys had tricked Caroline into believing that a skeleton of an abaguchie had been found in Oldakers' cellar.

When she had crawled down there to see the bones herself, without Mr. Oldaker's knowing, the boys had stood on the trapdoor so that she couldn't get back out. They had almost gotten in big, big trouble over that, and Wally wasn't about to have the same trick pulled on him.

But why would Mike Oldaker want to trick him?

"Wh-whose bones are they?" Wally asked.

"We don't know yet. But I'm counting on you to keep quiet about this," Mike said. "If you can keep a secret, then I'll see that your newspaper gets the scoop."

"But . . . But how are bones making that noise?" Wally whispered back.

This time Mike didn't answer. He just shook his head and walked away.

■ ■ ■ ■ ■ ■ ■ ■ ■ ■ ■ ■

Four

■

Roving Reporter

"Jake doesn't know what hit him!" Eddie said a few days later. "I've got him over a barrel. He'll have to do whatever I say." She was sprawled on the couch, papers scattered around her, and Caroline thought she looked a little too much like Cleopatra, sailing down the Nile on a royal boat.

This was Eddie at her worst, Caroline decided. Power sometimes went to her head.

Beth must have felt it too, because she said, "Being editor in chief doesn't just mean telling people what to do, Eddie. We've got to actually put out a newspaper, you know."

"I know. I'm working on the layout. As soon as I find out what each of you is going to write about, I can plan where to place each story."

"Well, I think I'll take the bike and ride around

town looking for an old haunted house," said Beth. "I'll ask at the shops on Main Street and see if anyone knows a good ghost story about a house here in Buckman."

"Take your camera, and if you find one, get a picture," Eddie said. "I'll see if I can scan it into the newspaper. We need to fill up as much space as possible. What about you, Caroline?"

"I'm going to the library and ask if they know someone I could interview about a dead relative," said Caroline.

"Now, listen," Eddie told her. "You can't just knock on someone's door and ask them about losing a brother or a grandfather or somebody. Don't forget to say, 'I'm sorry for your loss.' And make it sincere."

"You don't have to tell *me* how to act!" Caroline said hotly. "I can be the most sincerest person in the world, Eddie!" And Caroline put on her "tragic" face.

"Shove it," said Eddie.

Caroline found an old notebook from school, tore out the pages she had used, and, taking a pen, went downstairs. "I'm heading to the library, Mom," she called.

"All right," said Mrs. Malloy from the next room, where she was writing checks for the monthly bills. "You girls can make your own sandwiches for lunch. That and potato salad."

At the library, Caroline waited while a man asked the reference librarian where he could find information on box elder bugs. After the librarian had told him where to look, she turned to Caroline. "Are you interested in bugs too?" she asked, smiling.

"No, I'm writing obituaries," Caroline said.

"Excuse me?" said the librarian.

"I'm working on a historical newspaper with my sisters, and I want to interview the relatives of famous people from Buckman. Dead people, I mean."

"Well, I don't know that we've had any *really* famous people, but we certainly have had some interesting ones," the librarian said. "I can give you the names of several relatives, but I can't guarantee they'll want to talk to you."

"I understand," said Caroline, "and I'm sorry for their loss."

"All right," the librarian said. "Here are three people I happen to know personally, and it's quite all right to go inside their houses if they invite you. They all live within a few blocks of downtown." She wrote the names and addresses on a piece of paper and handed it to Caroline.

"Thank you," Caroline told her.

Outside, Caroline sat on the low stone wall and studied the piece of paper: *Ask Jim Hogan about his grandfather who fought in World War I,* the librarian had written. *Ask Sara Phillips about her aunt who made quilts. Ask Ms. Crane about her sister.*

Caroline started off. The first address was the downstairs apartment in a small, shingled house. When Caroline rang the bell, an elderly man using a walker came to the door. His white hair curled above his collar, and when he smiled, every wrinkle on his face seemed to have a proper place, as though the wrinkles were all a part of that smile.

"Hello. I'm Caroline Malloy and I've heard about your grandfather," Caroline began. "I'm sorry for your loss."

The smile on the man's face turned to surprise. "That was twenty-four years ago!" he said.

"Oh. Well, I'm working on a historical newspaper with my sisters, and the librarian said that maybe I could interview you for a story about your grandfather. I wondered if you could tell me what he did in the war," Caroline said.

"Well, why don't we just sit right here on the porch and I can tell you whatever you want to know," Mr. Hogan said.

Caroline had the feeling that perhaps Mr. Hogan was going to tell her more about the First World War than she wanted to know, and she was sure of it when, forty-five minutes later, her hand had grown tired from writing. She wished she had Beth's job instead, looking for haunted houses.

"So there he was in the trenches, artillery shells flying overhead, his canteen empty," Mr. Hogan went on, "when up in the sky he sees this American fighter plane taking out after the enemy. And all the soldiers on both sides, you know, are looking up from the trenches, watching the fight, and it's noon, you see, and—"

"Which reminds me," said Caroline, "I have two other people I need to interview today. I think maybe I'd better be going."

"Oh," said Mr. Hogan, sounding disappointed. "Well, you make sure I get a copy of your paper, now, when it comes out. And get his name right—Sergeant Oliver Raymond Hogan. . . ."

"Of course," said Caroline. "By the way, you wouldn't happen to know of any haunted houses in Buckman, would you?"

Mr. Hogan blinked. "Haunted houses? None that I can think of, though there were whispers going around when I was a little tyke that the old building where that bookstore is now was haunted. If my grandfather was alive, *he* could tell you."

"Thank you very much," said Caroline.

She went home for a sandwich, then set off again, looking for the next address on the slip of paper. She liked this job—liked being a roving reporter. But she wished she had taken the bike before Beth got it. At least on a bike you got a breeze. She wished, in fact, that for the moment she *was* Beth, looking up ghosts instead of obituaries. The sun bore down on her bare arms and legs, and Caroline stayed on the shady sides of the streets wherever she could.

At last she came to a redbrick house and knocked.

No one answered. Caroline knocked again, more loudly. Still no answer. She turned to go but then saw a car drive up. A woman got out and came toward the house, her arms loaded with groceries.

"Ms. Phillips?" Caroline asked, and took one of the bags from her. "Can I help?"

"Why, thank you," the woman said. "Were you waiting to see me?"

"I'm Caroline Malloy," Caroline told her, and explained about the newspaper.

Ms. Phillips smiled as she unlocked the door and led Caroline inside. "So you want to know more about my aunt," she said. "Well, why don't you come out to the kitchen and I'll tell you about her while I put the groceries away."

So Caroline sat on a high stool in Ms. Phillips's kitchen, notebook on her lap.

"You've probably heard that she loved to make quilts," Ms. Phillips told her. "She was forever collecting scraps of material to cut up into squares and triangles for her next quilt project. It got so that she always carried a trash bag around with her so that if anyone gave her an old apron to cut up or a flour sack or a sheet, she'd have something to put it in. People began affectionately calling her the bag lady because she took it everywhere she went and it never seemed to come back empty."

Caroline wrote the details down in her notebook but was dismayed to discover she was no more interested in quilts than she was in trenches and artillery shells.

"Why, Aunt Irene's quilts are all over town now," Ms. Phillips went on. "Each of her friends got one. The church got one to sell at their auction; the college got one; she even made quilts for the firehouse. When she died, we covered her casket with a quilt there at the funeral home to show how much we appreciated her."

"Was it buried with her?" asked Caroline.

"Excuse me?" said Ms. Phillips.

"I mean . . . the quilt . . . if you still have it . . . since it was on the casket . . . ," Caroline stammered, not knowing exactly *what* she meant, but imagining a ghost wrapped in a quilt standing there in the doorway.

"It was a perfectly lovely quilt and a lovely funeral," said Ms. Phillips, her eyes unsmiling.

"And it's a lovely story," said Caroline quickly. "I'm sorry for your loss."

"Thank you," said Ms. Phillips.

It was almost four o'clock when Caroline reached the last house—a huge white Victorian with green shutters. Maybe *this* could be the haunted house Beth was looking for. It wasn't until Caroline had un-latched the iron gate and started up the walk that she noticed a thin white-haired woman standing on the porch, arms folded across her brown dress, watching Caroline and frowning. She almost looked like a ghost herself.

"Well!" she said. "What took you so long?"

Caroline stared. *"What?"*

"My friend at the library called and said you wanted to talk to me about my sister," the woman said, but she seemed more friendly now that Caroline was up on the porch. "Do you like your iced tea with or without sugar?"

"Uh . . . with," Caroline said, and followed her inside.

It was obvious that the two sisters had lived together for a long time. The four walls of the living room were covered with photographs of the two girls in high school, of the two girls in secretarial school, of vacations taken together and birthday celebrations in this very house. *Tessie and Bessie, San Francisco, June 1951,* someone had written in a corner of one of the photographs. *Bessie and Tessie, Christmas, 1973.*

"Oh! You're looking at pictures of me and my sister," Ms. Crane said, coming back into the room with the tea, the ice clinking softly in the glasses. She gave Caroline a wink as she handed her the tea. "Pretty, isn't she?"

Caroline nodded and opened her notebook. A half hour later, she was still writing, and Ms. Crane was still talking.

"To tell the truth, she was a bit conceited," Ms. Crane went on. "Stuck on herself, you know. She had a beautiful party dress, and I asked once if I could wear it, but she wouldn't let me. Afraid I might be prettier in it than she was. Oh, and did she ever have a temper! I never told anyone before, but we used to fight like cats and dogs, and it was her who started it more often than not."

She stopped while Caroline finished writing a sentence, then continued: "I know you should speak well of the dead, and don't get me wrong—I loved my sister. But she was what she was, and she'd say the same of me. We had a lot of fun together, but she was a pill at times, and a nag as well, and grumpy as all get-out if she didn't get her way. Because we lived together our whole lives, people must have thought we got along like two peas in a pod, but let me tell you, it's hard sometimes to have your own identity when you've always lived with your sister."

Caroline was not about to ask Ms. Crane about ghosts here, because the house seemed creepy enough as it was, and the dead sister was all around them. So when the interview was over, she said simply, "Thank you for talking with me. I'm sorry for your loss."

"Well, don't be," said Ms. Crane, "because I'm getting along just fine by myself, if anyone wants to know."

As Caroline walked home, she decided she wouldn't want to live her whole life with her sisters. *She* certainly intended to have an identity of *her* own, because *her* name would be in lights on Broadway: *Caroline Lenore Malloy,* and it would be Beth and Eddie in the audience, admiring *her.*

"I don't think I'd want to live my whole life with you," she said to Eddie when she got home. Eddie was in the dining room working on a layout for the first issue.

Eddie placed one hand on her heart. "Oh, what a blow, Caroline!" she said. "I'm grief-stricken."

Caroline had started to tell her about Tessie and Bessie when they heard the clunk of the bike against the front steps and Beth burst through the front door.

"Eddie, do we have a name for our newspaper?" she panted.

"Not yet," said Eddie. "Why?"

"Because there are posters all over town, and you know what they say? *The Hatford Herald, Coming July Sixteenth, Eddie Malloy, Editor in Chief!*"

■ ■ ■ ■ ■ ■ ■ ■ ■ ■ ■

Five

■

The Secret

Ever since Wally's trip to Oldakers' Bookstore, he couldn't get those noisy bones off his mind.

You can't tell anyone, not even your brothers, Mike Oldaker had said. And Wally had nodded. He had said okay. It was the secret as much as the bones that worried him.

If he could keep a secret, Mike had promised, he would give the story to the *Hatford Herald* even before he told it to the *Buckman Bugle,* the city newspaper.

This was *big,* Wally thought. This was a *scoop*! This was absolutely, positively *huge*! Fantastic! All he had to do was not tell anybody, not even his parents.

He had always liked Mike because he seemed like a man who understood sitting on a porch and counting raindrops. Sitting on the steps studying an anthill. Floating bottles down a river or even spitting in the water from the footbridge. The kind of man who understood about lying in bed in the mornings trying to figure out where a spiderweb began.

But what was that scratching, scraping, clawing sound beneath the bookstore's floorboards? And why didn't Mike want anyone else to know? Was this about a murder? Wally wondered. Had the cellar been the scene of a crime, maybe, and somebody was down there covering up evidence? Or maybe those bones were alive! Maybe they were bones, all right, but they were covered by muscle and skin and hair! What if something, or someone, was being held prisoner down there? What if the bones got loose?

Okay, he said to himself, beginning to shiver. What did he really know about Mike Oldaker's cellar?

There were bones, Mike had said.

What had Wally *seen*?

Nothing.

What had he heard?

Scratching, clawing, scraping.

What did he really know about Mike Oldaker?

He owned the bookstore. He'd always seemed nice.

Nothing more.

■

The secret inside Wally Hatford was like a rock in his shoe. It was the first thing on his mind when he got up in the morning, the last thing he thought about before he went to sleep. The secret seemed to be growing bigger and bigger inside him, but he didn't tell a soul.

He tried to think of happy things instead. Christmas. Birthdays. Then he'd find himself thinking about that *scrape, scrape, claw, claw* sound underneath the floorboards in the bookstore. That store didn't seem to be such a comforting place anymore. Wally's own *house* didn't seem so comforting. Even his grandfather's portrait at the top of the stairs seemed to glower at him when he went to bed.

One night, Wally closed his eyes in the darkness and pulled the sheet up over his head. He tried to think of Christmas again, but his mind seemed to prefer Halloween. And then he was climbing down a ladder into a dark hole. Down . . . down . . . down . . . Colder, darker, spookier, creepier . . .

He found himself walking through a long dark tunnel, and there was a noise like hockey sticks clacking together. Up ahead he could see a far-off light, and with every step he took, the clacking sound grew louder.

Step by step . . . step by step . . .

Wally's heart began to pound. His pulse beat a little faster. His lips felt dry, and his palms began to sweat.

And suddenly he was in the room with the light, and there was a bucket of bones in the middle of the floor. The bones were moving! All at once they rose up out of the bucket and into the air. The knee bone connected to the thighbone, the thighbone connected to the hip bone, the hip bone connected to the backbone, the backbone connected to the neck bone, and—

"Arrrrggggghhhhh!" Wally yelled as something touched his forehead.

"Wally!" said his dad. "Wake up. You're having a bad dream."

"Whooooh!" gasped Wally.

"Are you awake? You okay?" asked Mr. Hatford.

"Whoooaaaah!" Wally bellowed.

"Wally, open your eyes. Sit up. Drink some water," said his dad.

Wally opened his eyes. He sat up. He was in his own room. There was a light on in the hall.

"You were yelling loudly enough to wake the dead," said Mr. Hatford.

Dead? "Whooooh!" Wally yelped again.

This time Mr. Hatford shook his shoulder. "Do you want to sleep with Peter for the rest of the night?" he asked.

"No," said Wally, his heart still racing.

"Count to five," said his father.

"One, two, three, four, five," said Wally.

"Where are you?"

"In the cellar," said Wally.

"No, you are right here in your own room, and I'm waiting for you to really wake up so *I* can go back to bed," said his dad.

"Good night," said Wally. "I'm okay."

Mr. Hatford went back to his own room, and Wally lay as still as a stone until his pulse returned to normal. This secret was too big to keep. This secret was going to drive him nuts.

And then he had a thought. Mike Oldaker had said that as soon as they found out who the bones belonged to, he'd tell Wally even before he called the *Buckman Bugle.*

If it had been a bad secret, an awful secret, Mike Oldaker would not have told Wally, and he certainly would not have been willing to tell the Buckman newspaper. Unless he was lying, of course.

Mike Oldaker had promised Wally a scoop, though, so for now, anyway, Wally was going to keep his mouth shut and see what happened.

■ ■ ■ ■ ■ ■ ■ ■ ■ ■ ■

Six

■

Psychic Energy

Eddie was spitting bullets. She leaped up from the table, scattering pencils and papers all over the floor. How dare the boys name the newspaper the *Hatford Herald*?

"I'm the editor in chief, and no one asked *me*!" she bellowed when Beth brought the news. "I never gave my okay!"

The posters were all around Buckman, Beth told her. The guys must have designed them on their computer, printed them up, and gone to every store downtown to put them in the shop windows.

"So what would you have named the paper?" Caroline asked, somewhat surprised at the uproar. What could you *expect* from a Hatford, after all?

"I don't know, but it wouldn't have *Hatford* in the title, you can be sure of that!" Eddie fumed. "The

Malloy Messenger! The *Girls' Dispatch!* The *Buckman Bulletin!* The *West Virginia Word! Anything* except the *Hatford Herald*. I wouldn't name it anything that even *smelled* of a boy!"

Caroline tried to figure that one out. She wondered if the Hatfords had an aura that she couldn't detect.

"Well, we can't do anything about it now," Beth said. "If you went around changing the posters, crossing out *Hatford Herald* and making it the *Malloy Messenger* or something, it would look like you're not really in charge, Eddie. Or that if you were, no one was paying attention."

Eddie growled in disgust.

"You'll just have to go along with it," Beth told her. "You'll have to pretend it was your idea too."

"What it means is we'll have to watch those guys like hawks to see what else they're up to," said Eddie, pacing back and forth like a tiger in a cage. "Why didn't *I* name the newspaper first? How could I have been so stupid?"

Caroline, however, was only half listening, because she saw the mail truck stop at the bottom of the driveway. She watched Mr. Hatford reach out and open the Malloys' box, put some mail inside, and turn up the red metal flag to show that there was mail.

Instantly, she was out the door and down the steps and was running down the long driveway toward the road. Mr. Hatford gave a soft toot of his horn as he drove away. When Caroline opened the box and found the envelope she had been waiting for, addressed to

Caroline Lenore Malloy, she took it up to her room before her sisters could see it.

Eddie and Beth were all wrapped up in making the newspaper, their father was in Ohio seeing about taking his old job again, and their mother was preoccupied with the possibility of moving. No one else in the family could ever understand the youngest Malloy daughter—*her*—she was sure of it. And of course Caroline didn't expect them to. No one else in the family wanted to go onstage, so this burden of being a misunderstood and unappreciated actress-in-the-making would be hers alone.

Caroline closed her bedroom door and eagerly tore open the envelope. There was the booklet she had seen advertised on the back of a movie magazine, a booklet for which she had paid two dollars and ninety-five cents plus postage: *Your Aura: Making It Work for You.*

What her family did not understand, Caroline told herself as she settled down in her chair by the window, was that actresses have to spend their whole lives getting people to pay attention to them. Once people stop paying attention, all the good roles in plays and movies go to someone else, and soon that actress is only a has-been. If Greta Garbo and Katharine Hepburn and Helen Hayes had an aura, there was no reason why Caroline Lenore Malloy shouldn't have one too. She believed in working hard for what she wanted, and an aura just might help.

Caroline opened the booklet to the first page: *An aura is psychic energy drawn from the soul, which radiates out to other people and alerts them to your presence,* she read.

Caroline reached for the package of corn chips she kept in a drawer and popped one into her mouth. Then another and another as she read on:

An aura broadcasts a woman's intelligence, beauty, sensitivity, and passion. A light scarf worn over the head will contain the aura until the desired moment is at hand. Once the scarf is removed and the aura is released, replace the head scarf and repeat the following exercises. . . .

Caroline read about the position in which she should be sitting, the manner in which her fingertips should be touching, the thoughts she should be thinking, and whether her eyes were to be open or closed. The hum, of course, was her own idea.

Half an hour later, Eddie peeped into the room and found Caroline sitting cross-legged on her bed with a thin white curtain draped over her head. She was humming one long, low note.

"Caroline, what the heck?" Eddie said.

When Caroline didn't answer, didn't even open her eyes, Eddie went over to the bed and picked up the booklet in her sister's lap: " '. . . psychic energy drawn from the soul, which radiates out to other people . . .'," she read aloud. "Caroline, where do you get this stuff? It's unscientific! Utter nonsense!"

"Well, it's true, Eddie, or it wouldn't be in print," Caroline said, peeping out from under the curtain.

"Just because something's in print doesn't make it true," Eddie told her. "I could write that the Hatford boys were the smartest people on the planet, but that wouldn't make it true."

"Then why would someone bother to print up this booklet?" asked Caroline.

"Because you and a thousand others were willing to send them two dollars and ninety-five cents," said Eddie.

But Caroline wanted to believe she had an aura, and when Eddie went back downstairs, Caroline went right on humming.

She took a break for lunch, then seated herself on the living room rug, this time using the short plastic "psychic stick" that had come with the booklet. While she hummed, she traced a line all the way up one side of her body, from her ankle to her armpit. First the right side, then the left, just as the booklet instructed.

"Will you *stop*?" Beth cried out as she stumbled over Caroline again. "Take your aura and your Oreos or whatever, and go someplace else, Caroline!"

All right, Caroline thought. She knew when she wasn't wanted. She put the booklet away till after dinner, and then, because she knew she might be asked to wash the dishes if she stuck around, she took her booklet, her psychic stick, and her curtain down to the big rock on the Malloys' side of the river so that she could practice undisturbed. If her father did move the family back to Ohio, wouldn't it be great to return to school with an aura? To have everyone notice her and wonder how she got to be so special?

Caroline climbed up on the rock. Lights were beginning to come on in houses across the river, and fireflies flickered in the dark trees. Caroline sat perfectly straight on the rock, her fingertips touching. She had slipped off her sandals and tried to sit so that the soles of her feet were touching. Then, with the curtain draped over her head, she closed her eyes and hummed a long, low note. Whenever she ran out of breath, she took a quick gulp of air and went on humming, helping her psychic energy to escape her scalp but trapping it under the curtain until she could go back to the house, remove the curtain, and see whether her family turned around to look before they even heard her coming.

A twig snapped.

Caroline opened her eyes and tried to see through the curtain, but she did not move her head.

There was rustling in the bushes.

Silence.

And then, a few moments later, the sound of feet pounding down the path to the river and the bouncing and creaking of the swinging bridge.

Seven

■

Gone

Wally was making himself a milk shake. A super-thick chocolate milk shake, one so thick that a straw would stand straight up in it. A *spoon* could stand up in it, in fact. A milk shake so chocolatey that it was as dark as the brown shoes he wore on Sundays.

He poured one-fourth cup of milk into the blender. He added one-fourth cup of cream. Three scoops of chocolate ice cream. Two tablespoons of chocolate syrup.

What else? Wally wandered around the kitchen. He found two packages of cocoa mix and dumped those in the blender.

What else? A banana. A teaspoon of vanilla. A teaspoon of honey. His eye fell on the peanut butter jar, and he scooped up a huge spoonful and held it over the blender.

The phone rang, and Wally picked it up with his other hand.

"Wally," said his mother, who worked at the hardware store. "This is my night to work late, so I'm going to dash home around five-thirty and make a quick supper before I go back. I want you boys to stick to fruit for snacks this afternoon so you'll be hungry for an early dinner, okay?"

Plop! The glob of peanut butter left the spoon and landed in the blender, splattering the countertop.

"Okay," said Wally.

After he hung up, he put the lid back on the blender and turned the appliance on. The blades got stuck in the peanut butter. He took the lid off, poked around to mix it up, then turned the blender on again. One minute . . . two minutes . . . three minutes. When he was done, his straw stuck straight up in the mixture, and a spoon leaned only a little to one side.

Wally poured the milk shake into a glass and sat down at the kitchen table. This was paradise. This was what summer was all about. This milk shake was so good, thought Wally, it could be sold for five dollars in New York City! Ten, even! Why, he could go into business! If he couldn't think of any other job to do when he grew up, he would move to New York and start a chocolate-peanut-butter-banana milk shake business for all the people who worked in the Empire State Building.

"Wall-*ly*!" yelled Jake from upstairs. "How do you spell *judgment*? Is there an *e* after the *g*?"

"No," Wally called back, and hunkered down a little farther in his chair. *Slurp.* He took a long swallow, filling his mouth with the chocolate stuff. One taste of this was almost better than Christmas and birthdays and Halloween put together!

"What about *cancellation?*" Jake yelled. "One *l* or two?"

Wally sighed. "Two," he called. Each word popped up on a billboard in his brain. He never forgot.

At last all the creamy goodness was gone and Wally gave a contented belch. He wiped his mouth and took his glass to the sink. He rinsed and dried the blender. He rinsed and dried the spoon and glass. He threw away the straw and wiped the countertop.

When Josh came into the kitchen looking for a snack, Wally said, "Mom says not to eat anything but fruit until suppertime."

"Darn!" said Josh, and reluctantly picked up an apple.

Wally went into the living room and lay down on the couch, hands on his stomach, a smile on his face.

■

Mrs. Hatford was impressed.

"I'm really happy that you boys are doing something productive this summer!" she said as she passed a platter of cheeseburgers. Josh took two, Jake took three; Wally took one and asked Peter if he wanted half.

Potato salad came next, and Wally took a tablespoonful. Same with cole slaw.

"Wally Hatford, what did you have to eat this afternoon?" his mother asked.

"I didn't eat anything," Wally said, which was the

truth in a way because you don't eat a milk shake, you drink it. "I just had a really big drink. I guess that filled me up."

Mr. Hatford was reading the article Jake had written about a college football game back in 1948.

"This is interesting!" he said. "I think a lot of old-timers are going to enjoy your newspaper, boys. Could be that some of the folks around here remember that quarterback."

"I'm helping with the newspaper too, but they haven't given me a job yet," Peter complained. "They never let me do anything!"

"Tell you what," said Josh. "You can go with Wally to take my cartoon over to the Malloys' this evening. Eddie's going to scan it into the newspaper."

Wally bristled. "Why am *I* the one who has to deliver it to Eddie? Why don't you take it over yourself?"

"You agreed to be the distributor, didn't you?" said Jake. "Well . . . *distribute!*"

Wally sighed. Okay. All he had to do was walk across the footbridge, go up the hill, knock on the Malloys' back door, and see that Eddie got the cartoon. He didn't have to say anything but "Here. Take it." He could be polite without having to be nice. Before any of the girls could say something at all that might lead to trouble, he would be home again, and no ghostly presence would find anything to hold against him.

It was almost eight-fifteen when Josh finished his cartoon, and it took fifteen minutes more to draw a decoration to go with Jake's football story.

"If you want to go with me, Peter, get your shoes on," Wally called.

Peter came clumping down the stairs in his sneakers, the laces flopping.

"Tie them," said Wally. "You'll trip."

"Huh-*uh*!" Peter said. "I learned how not to trip on my shoelaces."

"How's that?"

"You walk with your legs apart," Peter said, and demonstrated, teetering from side to side as the boys went down the front steps.

"Tie them!" Wally said.

Peter sighed. "O-*kay*," he said, and knelt down to do it.

Dusk was settling in over the river, and pinpoints of fireflies sparkled along the bank. For some reason, Peter always spoke in a whisper when they were out at night, and he was whispering now.

"What if two of those fireflies were really wolf eyes looking at us, Wally?" he asked.

"There aren't any wolves in Buckman," said Wally, whispering back without knowing why.

"That's what they said about a cougar, until they knew what it was," said Peter. They continued on a little way and then he asked, "What about ghosts? Do ghosts eat people?"

Why did reminders of ghosts keep coming at him from all sides? Wally wondered. He had sat down the other night to watch a movie called *The Fog People* with Jake and Josh. Only Wally had thought they had said

The Frog People. He had thought it was going to be about aliens, but it wasn't. It was about ghosts. It scared him almost as much as the library book had, but the twins would have teased him if he'd gotten up and left the room.

"What made you think about ghosts?" asked Wally, his skin beginning to crawl.

"Because it's the ghost hour. They come out at dark, right?"

"You don't believe that, do you?" Wally asked.

"Yep," said Peter.

"Well, they don't eat people. They don't have stomachs. They don't even have mouths. That's why they're ghosts."

Peter looked relieved.

The fact was, if that story in the library book was true, which it wasn't, there were ghostly presences all around. *He* had a ghostly self. *Peter* had a ghostly self. And maybe, if he just narrowed his eyes and stared hard at Peter, walking on ahead, he could make out a sort of mist or cloud bobbing along above him. Wally narrowed his eyes and stared as hard as he could. Nothing.

The swinging bridge swayed as they started across. Peter ran his hand along the rope railing, taking it away each time they reached a support cable, then putting his hand back again. He counted each cable: "One . . . two . . . three . . ."

When they got to the other side, both boys cast wary glances at the tall brush on either side of the path that led up the hill to the Malloys' backyard. Peter moved a little closer to Wally's leg.

Suddenly Wally slowed and listened, his head cocked to one side. He heard something but couldn't tell what. It sounded like a small motor. A long, low hum that was strung out for fourteen or fifteen seconds. Then, after a short pause, it continued on the same note.

Peter heard it too. Hesitantly, they started forward again, heads turning right and left to see if they could tell where the sound was coming from.

Then Wally came to a dead stop and grabbed Peter's arm. For there, on the big rock on this side of the river, was a white apparition. A strange unearthly hum was coming from the ghostlike figure. Wally couldn't tell whether it was male or female, human or beast. It was covered with a thin white film that fluttered slightly in the breeze.

Wally thought of the ghost in his summer reading book; the fog people in the movie, with their long fingers that you could see right through; the mysterious scratching, clawing, scraping sound beneath the floorboards in Mike Oldaker's cellar. Suddenly he felt his feet turning, his legs moving, and before he knew it he was back on the swinging bridge heading for home at breakneck speed.

When he collapsed on the porch and turned to ask Peter if he had seen it too, Peter was not there. Peter had disappeared.

Eight

■

Peter Squeals

Now what? Caroline wondered, looking around. Maybe her aura was working and she was attracting people already.

It sounded as though someone had started up the path, then stopped, then run back over the footbridge again. Probably one of the Hatford boys spying on her, as usual. Caroline reached up and pulled the curtain off her head. There stood Peter Hatford, staring at her.

"I *thought* it was you," he said.

"Really?" said Caroline. "Did you sense something unusual in the atmosphere, Peter?"

"No," said Peter. "I saw your shoes beside the rock."

"Oh," said Caroline, disappointed.

"Why do you have a curtain over your head?" asked Peter.

"It's a shawl," said Caroline. "So who else is hanging around over here? Wally? The twins?"

"Wally thought you were a ghost, I think," said Peter. "He went home."

Caroline laughed. "So where were you going?"

"To your place," said Peter. "I guess I'll have to go by myself."

"I guess so," said Caroline. She slid down off the rock and picked up her sandals. She'd have to work on her aura another time, because it was always fun when Peter came over. He could be bribed with a couple of cookies to tell the girls almost anything they wanted to know. He followed her up to the house.

"Peter's here," Caroline called out as they went through the back door. Eddie and Beth were finishing the dinner dishes, and Caroline knew she'd have to do them the next night.

Beth grinned at Eddie. "And I wonder what *he* wants?" she murmured, hanging up the dish towel.

Peter walked over to the table and waited expectantly.

"So what's up, Peter?" said Eddie.

"Nothing," said Peter. "I'm helping Wally. We were bringing over the cartoon Josh drew for the newspaper."

"Yeah? Where is it?" asked Eddie.

"Wally's got it."

"So did he fall off the bridge or what?" asked Beth.

"I think he got scared by Caroline with the curtain over her head," said Peter, his eyes traveling around the kitchen until they came to rest on the cookie canister.

"She's enough to scare anybody, curtain or no curtain," said Eddie. "What kind of cartoon did he draw?"

"I don't know," said Peter. "I just came along to keep Wally company."

"Uh-huh," said Eddie, and she and Beth and Caroline exchanged smiles.

Beth leaned against the kitchen counter, arms folded over her chest. "Well, I don't know if we have any cookies for you or not, Peter."

"Yeah. We can't give you cookies for *nothing*," said Eddie. "But maybe we could find some if you give us information in return."

Peter sighed. "What kind of information?" he asked.

"Oh, any *other* secret plans your brothers might have for the newspaper," Eddie said. "It was a dirty rotten trick to name the newspaper the *Hatford Herald* and put posters all over town without telling us."

"Yeah. That's what Jake said you'd say," said Peter.

"So is there anything else we don't know about?"

Peter thrust his hands into his pockets and frowned thoughtfully. "Like an ace in the hole?" he asked.

"Exactly," said Eddie.

Peter frowned some more. "What kind of cookies?"

Beth reached around for the canister and checked. "Peanut butter chocolate chunk, your favorite kind."

"Okay," said Peter.

"First," said Eddie, "what have Jake and Josh and

Wally said about us? Are they okay with me being editor in chief?"

Peter climbed onto a kitchen stool. "I don't think so," he said. "Jake isn't, anyway."

"No? What has he said?"

Beth dug into the canister and held up a large cookie studded with chunks of dark chocolate. Eddie poured Peter a glass of milk.

Peter squirmed hard and pursed his mouth, trying to remember. "Um . . . he said . . . 'That old hotshot Eddie doesn't know about our ace in the hole if she gets too bossy.'"

"Yeah? And what would that be?" Eddie said, putting the milk down in front of Peter.

"How many cookies do I get?" asked Peter.

"Three," said Beth.

"Four," said Peter.

"Okay, four. Now what's their ace in the hole, Peter? What would they do?" Eddie asked.

"Strike," said Peter, and took the first cookie.

Beth and Eddie and Caroline all stared at Peter.

"Strike?" said Eddie. "Hey, *we're* not the ones who are getting summer reading credit for making a newspaper. We'll probably be back in Ohio by September."

Peter shrugged. "That's what he said. Strike." He swung his legs back and forth while he chewed. Beth put three more cookies on a saucer and set it before him.

"The problem," Beth said, thinking it over, "is that

your name is on it as editor in chief, Eddie. If the paper doesn't come out . . ."

"It'll come out if we have to do it all ourselves!" Eddie said hotly. "Besides, who said I'm bossy? Who said I'm not fair? I can be the unbossiest, most fair person in the world when I want to be."

"That's good," said Peter, swinging his legs some more.

"Hello, Peter," Mrs. Malloy said, coming into the kitchen with a pan full of peas she had been shelling in front of the TV. "How are things at your house?"

"Sort of boring," said Peter. "I'm supposed to have a job on the newspaper and nobody lets me do any work."

"Poor thing," said Beth.

"Are you going to miss us if we move back to Ohio?" Mrs. Malloy teased.

Peter nodded.

"What will you miss the most?" asked Beth.

Peter looked down at the cookies in front of him and everyone laughed.

"I thought so," said Eddie.

The phone rang just then and Caroline answered. It was Wally.

"Is . . . is Peter there?" he asked.

"Peter . . . ?" Caroline paused, smiling at her sisters. "Why? Is he missing?"

"Caroline!" her mother said sternly.

"Yes, he's here," said Caroline.

Now it was Jake on the phone. "Let me speak to Peter," he said.

"He's got a mouthful of cookies, sorry," said Caroline.

"Well, tell him to swallow," said Jake.

Caroline turned to Peter. "Swallow," she said.

Peter did. Then he drank some milk and took another bite.

"Okay, he's listening," Caroline said, and held the phone up to Peter's ear, but far enough away that she and her sisters could hear too.

"Peter!" said Jake. "Don't tell the girls anything. Do you hear me?"

Peter nodded.

"Are you listening, Peter?"

"Uh-huh," said Peter, and went on chewing.

"*Any*thing!" Jake repeated. "Josh will take his cartoon over there tomorrow and you come on home. Now! And keep your mouth shut."

"Okay," said Peter.

Mrs. Malloy put the peas in the refrigerator for the next day's dinner. "Caroline, when Peter finishes eating, walk him home, will you? He shouldn't be crossing that bridge in the dark by himself. Take a flashlight."

Peter finished the last cookie and rubbed his stomach contentedly.

"Come on," said Caroline, and he followed her outside.

They went back down the path to the river, the beam from the flashlight leading the way. Caroline took the opportunity to ask, "If we move back to Ohio, Peter, what will you remember most about me?"

"I don't know," said Peter.

"Well, think. Does anything in particular come to mind? My face? My voice? My hair? My eyes?"

"Your elbows," said Peter.

Caroline stopped and stared at him. "My *elbows*?"

"Yeah," said Peter. "They're sort of dirty. I think you lean your arms on the paper when you read the comics or something. Wally does the same thing and he gets dirty elbows too."

Caroline did not care to walk Peter across the bridge. She shone the flashlight on the wooden planks till he was safely on the other side, and waited until she heard the door slam in the house across the river. Then she turned and went back home.

Her elbows! All this time she'd been going around with ink smudges on her elbows! The embarrassment! The humiliation! Now she'd have to do something really spectacular so that people would forget all about her elbows!

■ ■ ■ ■ ■ ■ ■ ■ ■ ■ ■

Nine

■

The *Old Times Tribune*

Wally was ashamed of himself. He had not meant to leave Peter behind. He had not even meant to run. He was enormously relieved when he called the Malloys and found out that Peter was there—eating cookies, as usual—but he was embarrassed to tell his brothers how it had happened. About all the ghosts that had taken a room in his brain.

"Don't ever leave Peter alone with those girls, not even for a second!" Jake said. "You can never trust him to keep his mouth shut."

"So what's there to tell?" Wally asked.

"You never know, where Peter's concerned. He picks up things like you wouldn't believe," said Jake.

So when the door banged and Peter finally came in, the three boys descended on him and spirited him away upstairs. They sat him on one of the beds in the twins' room.

"What did you do at the Malloys?" Josh asked.

Peter still had crumbs on his T-shirt. "Ate cookies," he said, and held up four fingers.

"So what was on the rock?" asked Wally.

"Caroline. With a curtain over her head," said Peter.

Wally felt his cheeks grow warm. *Doubly* embarrassing. He had run all the way home because of *that*? It was useless, of course, to ask why Caroline had had a curtain over her head. It was useless to ask why Caroline did any of the things she did.

"Well, she sure fooled you, Wally," said Josh. "What did you think she was? A ghost? Peter didn't run."

" 'Cause I saw her shoes. I knew it was Caroline," Peter told them.

Wally hadn't seen any shoes.

"So how did you get inside their house, Peter?" asked Jake.

"Walked."

"We *know* you walked! I mean, what did you have to do to get cookies?"

Peter shrugged.

"Did they ask you any questions?" Josh wanted to know.

"I guess so," said Peter.

"What?"

"They wanted to know if you liked the idea of Eddie being editor in chief, and I said, 'Not much.' "

"Yeah? What else?"

Peter shrugged again, this time holding his shoulders high for a second or two before he dropped them.

"What *else*?" Jake insisted.

"I didn't say we would go on strike," said Peter.

"Well, we *won't* unless we have to," said Jake. "What *did* you say?"

"I just said that was our ace in the hole."

"Arrrrrgggghhhh!" cried Jake. "Peter, we're trying for once to get along with the Malloys because we need to get this newspaper out. That'll just make them mad! We should never have let you out of the house."

"We should never have let you be part of the newspaper," added Josh.

Peter was on the verge of tears. "Well, I'm *not* a part of the newspaper!" he said. "You didn't give me anything to do."

Wally felt sorry for his brother. It was *Wally's* fault that Peter had been left behind, and that Caroline had taken him up to the house.

"It's okay, Peter," he said. "I'm going to make you my assistant, as long as you don't go back to the Malloys' till after the newspaper comes out."

"Okay," said Peter. "So what's my job?"

"You're the ADM—assistant distribution manager," said Wally.

Peter was happy.

■

The following day Josh himself turned in his cartoon, and Wally took Peter with him to Oldakers'

Bookstore. He didn't tell Peter why he was going, though. He said they were going to look at comic books, but Wally wondered whether he would hear the thumps and scrapes and scratchings coming from the cellar, as he had before. And, if he did, whether he could figure out what they were. And whether Mike Oldaker could tell him now what it was all about.

"How are you doing, Wally?" Mike asked when the two boys walked through the door.

"Okay," said Wally, alert for the slightest noise coming from below.

There was a story hour going on for younger children, however, and they were all hooting and laughing at the tale, which made softer sounds impossible to hear. While Peter went over to listen to the story, Wally moved slowly down the aisles, looking through books on survival and adventure.

Mike must have known that Wally particularly liked nonfiction. "We've got a new book in on early natives of North America, Wally," he said. "And another one, on the top shelf there, on whales. Both of them are good."

Well, maybe, thought Wally. But what about a book on *ghosts* of North America? That would be more like it. What about a story of the haunted bookstores of West Virginia? About owners who kept bones beneath the floorboards?

"By the way," Mike went on. "Two other boys from your school were in here yesterday. They said they're going to put out a newspaper too. Calling it the *Old*

Times Tribune. Just thought you'd like to know you've got some competition. Haven't heard of anyone else doing a paper, though."

"Are you going to keep a stack of their papers here too?" Wally asked.

"Sure. Why not? As long as they do a good job." Then Mike winked. "Don't worry," he said in a low voice. "Your paper will still get the scoop when it's time."

But when would it be time? Wally wanted to ask.

Story hour was over, and the noisy children were spreading out all over the store. Peter came looking for Wally, and they browsed through the comic books, hunting for Peter's favorites.

When most of the other children had left and the bookstore was quiet again, Wally listened, and sure enough, he heard a faint scratching and clawing from below.

He looked at Peter to see whether he had noticed. Peter had his nose buried in a book.

I know something else is down there, and it's not just bones, Wally told himself as they left the store and started for home. What if Mike was just feeding *him* a story—making him think that he'd tell Wally the secret when the time was right, and it turned out that the time would never be right? That he'd never planned to give their newspaper, or any other newspaper, "the scoop"? That when the secret *did* get out, it would be horrible, and it would also be too late?

Wally didn't tell his brothers this, of course. He had

a different sort of news for them. "There's another history newspaper now called the *Old Times Tribune*," he said. "Two guys from our school, Mike said."

Jake thought it over. "Well, it's no skin off our nose," he said. "There could be a dozen newspapers for all we care. We just have to make sure ours is the best."

"Why?" asked Wally.

"Why? *Because!*" said Jake, as though that were the answer. With Jake, everything had to be a contest. There had to be a winner. And the only possible winner, as far as Jake was concerned, was Jake Hatford.

Wally wanted to tell him not to worry, because they were going to get a big scoop. They were going to get a story that not even the *Buckman Bugle* would report first. But he couldn't say a word. About Mike Oldaker. About the scratching and clawing. About the bones in the cellar. Not a word.

■ ■ ■ ■ ■ ■ ■ ■ ■ ■

Ten

■

Ghostly Gray

"I found one!"

Beth jumped off the bike, dropped it on the grass, and ran over to where Caroline and Eddie were taking turns on the rope swing. The large beech tree in the front yard provided a cool resting place between turns.

"One what?" asked Eddie.

"An old haunted house for my story!" said Beth. "Come and see. It's just on the other side of the business district."

Beth had been disappointed in her search for a haunted house. Everyone she had talked to seemed to know of some place that was haunted, but none of those places looked spooky enough, Beth had told her sisters. What was spooky about a bank building, a bookstore, a library, a small brick house? All it took, it seemed, for a place to be called haunted was for someone to die there at one time or another. That hardly made it haunted. But now she'd found one.

"It's too hot to look at houses now, Beth, and it's getting hotter," said Eddie. "Wait till the sun goes down. We'll walk over after dinner."

"All right. I'm taking my camera, too. I'd love to get a really spooky picture. Will you put it on the front page?"

"Depends," said Eddie. "I want to read your story first. Did someone tell you a story about a ghost in that house or something?"

"No, but I'm working on it," said Beth.

"Well, make sure the house is *old.* This is supposed to be a newspaper about houses that are *historical,* not *haunted.* But of course, if they could be both . . ."

The girls went over to sit on the porch steps.

"Let's figure out what we have for the newspaper so far," Eddie continued. "I'm doing a story on the swinging bridges of Buckman; you're doing old houses, Beth; Caroline's doing the Bessie-Tessie Crane story; Jake's writing up an old college football game; and Josh is doing a cartoon about what Buckman was like before air-conditioning. We're going to need more, you know, if we expect to fill up three issues."

"I know!" said Caroline. "I could do a story on the first theater in Buckman, and then tell how a future actress is living here right this very minute!"

"You, of course. Yeah, right," said Eddie.

"Really, Eddie! I could do a good job with it! We could tie in past and present and future, all in the same article!" Sometimes Caroline was so precocious she surprised even herself.

"Well, go ahead and write it, Caroline, but I won't promise to print it. Let's see how it turns out."

"Eddie!" Mrs. Malloy called from inside. "Jake's on the phone."

The girls scrambled up and went indoors. All three listened in.

"Just thought you'd like to know we've got some competition," Jake said. "Wally was at the bookstore and found out that some other guys are doing a newspaper. They're calling it the *Old Times Tribune*."

"So?" said Eddie. "Maybe everybody in the whole class will do newspapers. What do we care?"

Caroline and Beth grinned at each other. The reason Jake cared was that everything he did had to be a contest.

"Listen," Eddie went on. "Forget the other newspaper. I read your write-up of the football game, and it's pretty good. You guys want to go with us to see a haunted house after dinner? Beth's doing a story on old houses of Buckman and she thinks she's found one that's haunted."

"How would you know whether it's haunted or not?" Jake asked.

"I don't know. I guess that's up to Beth. You want to go or not?"

"Yeah, we'll go."

"Meet us at the drugstore at eight," Eddie said.

■

Caroline had found a picture of the actress Shirley Temple. She had dimples and very curly hair, and she was wearing a necklace of tiny stones. Caroline put on a necklace, unfastened her ponytail, and tried to twist her long hair into curls. She stuck a finger in each cheek to see how she would look with dimples. She didn't look much like Shirley.

"Caroline, are you coming or not?" Beth called from the front hall.

The haunted house! Caroline put down her brush and clattered downstairs. She wasn't trying to *look* like Shirley Temple, exactly. She was just trying to figure out what helped make an aura. Dimples didn't seem to help.

"So what are you all fixed up for?" Eddie asked, noticing Caroline's attempt at curls. "Trying to make yourself look good for *Walll-ly?*"

"Bleagh!" said Caroline, pretending to throw up.

"Josh? Jake?" Eddie teased. "Or is it *Peter?*"

"A *house* won't care how you look, Caroline," said Beth.

"None of the above," said Caroline. "I was just trying on a new look."

At eight o'clock, the three girls walked up the sidewalk to the drugstore, where the four boys were waiting. Peter was leaping over cracks in the sidewalk, first one way, then the other. From a distance he looked like a jumping frog.

"Wally said I could come too," Peter told them. "I'm his assistant."

"Good for you," said Eddie.

It seemed strange to be going somewhere with the Hatfords, Caroline thought as they all crowded onto the sidewalk and started toward the other end of town.

"The house is perfect!" Beth was saying. "It looks spooky even in the morning in the bright sun."

"So how do you know it's haunted?" asked Wally.

"I've talked with the family next door," said Beth. "They don't know who the house belongs to. They've never seen anyone go in or out. It's obviously abandoned, so it *might* be haunted."

Caroline could understand her sister's logic. When Beth got going, she had a wild imagination too, and if there wasn't a story to go along with that house, she'd *make* one!

"Wow!" said Peter.

"The grass is unmowed, the windows are dirty! I've got fast film in my camera, and hope I can get a good picture," Beth said. "It sure looks a lot more haunted than some of the other stuff people told me about."

"*What* other stuff?" asked Wally.

"The library, the bank building, the bookstore . . . ," said Beth.

"The *bookstore*?" Wally said, turning in her direction.

"Don't get your pants in an uproar," said Beth. "Some people think that almost anything over fifty years old around here is haunted."

"But how do you know it's really old?" asked Eddie.

"You can tell just by looking. The neighbors said it's the architecture of the late 1890s," said Beth.

They crossed at the corner, passed the dry cleaners, and marched on toward the supermart.

"What do you suppose the *Old Times Tribune* is going to write about?" asked Josh. "I hope they don't try to steal any of our ideas."

"They won't even *know* any of our ideas, because we're not going to tell them," said Jake.

The sun was low, but the air didn't seem that much cooler. It was humid, and there wasn't even a wisp of a breeze. Caroline felt a thin trickle of perspiration roll down the middle of her back.

"Okay, now," Beth said finally, when they had gone almost a mile. "It's on the next block, the house at the very end."

The sky was turning purple and gray when the house loomed up before them. It, too, was gray, and the Hatfords and the Malloys simply stood and stared.

This was a part of town that even Jake and Josh didn't know very well. The houses here were farther apart than they were on the other side of the business district—and old. Definitely old.

The big house with the peeling gray paint sat back from the street. One of the shutters had come loose and hung at an angle. The fence in front was falling down, and old newspapers and leaves had blown up against the remaining posts. No car was parked in the driveway. No light came from any of the windows.

"You're sure no one is there?" said Josh.

"See for yourself! It's deserted!" said Beth.

Josh opened the gate. "Let's go take a look," he said.

It was a corner house, so there was open space on one side of it. Beth led the way up the crumbling walk to the porch.

"Be careful," she warned, testing with her foot. "One of these boards is loose."

The porch creaked as the seven moved over to a window. Caroline could see some furniture inside. A tall upright piano. A worn couch. An old-fashioned lamp. An armchair.

"It looks like one day they all disappeared and left things just the way they were," said Eddie.

Back down the steps they went so that Beth could take a picture in the fading light, and then they trooped around back. There were cobwebs and more leaves on the back porch, and mice had made a nest in a flowerpot.

"So where does the ghost come in, Beth?" asked Wally. "Has anyone seen it yet?"

"I'm still working on that," said Beth. "But it wouldn't surprise me if the family moved away because of it. I mean, why else would a family move and not take anything? Why else wouldn't they tell their neighbors goodbye? If we move back to Ohio, *we'll* say goodbye."

"Beth, you've got to have more proof than that!" Eddie said. "You can't just say there's a ghost because it wouldn't surprise you if there was one! Come on. We'd better go."

Night was coming on fast, as it always did in West Virginia. Once the sun went down behind the hills, it was as though the mountains had swallowed it up. In a little while it would be dark.

They walked around to the front again and started for the gate, but Caroline wanted one more look at the old piano and chair, at the worn velvet couch with a picture above it. She ran up on the front porch and over to the window.

But this time, when she looked inside, she screamed. Because, for just a moment, she saw the ghostly figure of a young girl looking back.

■ ■ ■ ■ ■ ■ ■ ■ ■ ■

Eleven

■

Letter to Georgia

Dear Bill (and Danny and Steve and Tony and Doug):

What are you guys doing down there in Georgia anyway that's so important you can't move back here till September? I thought that once school was out, you couldn't wait to get back to West Virginia. You haven't gone and fallen in love with any Georgia peaches, have you?

So do you know how I'm spending July? I'm a distributor, that's what. Jake and Josh get credit toward their summer reading list if they put out three issues of a newspaper. It has to be about historical Buckman, and somehow Peter and I got roped into helping out. As if that's not bad enough, Jake—Jake!—asked the Malloy girls to go in on it with us. Big mistake. Eddie named herself editor in chief, of course, so Jake tricked her and named the paper the Hatford Herald *before she knew anything about it. Expect major explosions in the upper atmosphere.*

Tonight we went to see a house that Beth thinks is haunted, and just before we left, Caroline says she saw the ghost of a girl looking back at her. Is she crazy or is she nuts? Or . . . are there things here in Buckman we never knew about?

Mr. Malloy's gone to Ohio to see if he wants his old job back as football coach. He'd better take it, because they've got to be out of your house by the time you guys come back.

It can't be too soon for me.

Wally (and Jake and Josh and Peter)

P.S. Don't ever read a book called A Ghost's Revenge. Don't ever watch a movie called The Fog People. Not unless you want to be scared out of your socks and underwear!

Twelve

■

Caroline Pickford

Caroline lay on her bed, a booklet propped up on her stomach. She was learning all sorts of things about auras. The booklet had a drawing of a woman's head with a sort of halo around it.

An arrow led from the space inside the halo to some print off to one side.

Innermost aura, it read. *Natural protection force field.*

Beyond the first halo was another. An arrow to the space under *that* halo pointed to the words *Midsection aura: recent emotions and current well-being.*

The space beneath a third halo was labeled *Early memories and past lives.* Each of these three sections had colors, the booklet said. With practice, a person could learn to interpret another person's mood by the color of his aura, and thereby learn to get along better with those around him.

Caroline was not sure she believed in past lives, but if she'd had one, she was sure she had been an actress.

"Caroline!" came Eddie's voice from below. "Are you going to help out on this newspaper or not?"

Eddie sure was getting crabby lately, Caroline thought. Why did she want to be editor in chief anyway? Just so she could boss everyone around?

"Coming!" Caroline called.

She got up off her bed and went downstairs. The dining room had been transformed into a newspaper office. The long table was covered with notebooks and paper and pencils and scissors. Eddie had taped a piece of paper to the wall, and on it she had written: *first issue, July 16; second issue, July 23; third issue, July 30.*

"So what do you want me to do?" Caroline asked.

"We need someone to go to the library and get an early map of the city. If this is going to be a historical newspaper, we should have an old map or drawing or sketch or *some*thing to put in the paper," Eddie told her.

"Okay, I'll go," said Caroline, noting that Beth was hard at work on her haunted house story.

"Make a copy of the downtown area of any old map you can find and I'll scan it into our paper," said Eddie. "And while you're at it, think of something else you can write about. I've got your Tessie and Bessie Crane story, but we still need more. Go ahead and do that story about the first theater in Buckman if you want. We're really hurting for material here."

"The article about the first theater in Buckman and

the aspiring young actress who happens to be living here right now?" Caroline asked eagerly.

"Yeah, yeah, yeah—just make sure that ninety percent of the article is about the theater, Caroline, and only ten percent is about you."

At last! thought Caroline. *Publicity! The first thing an actress needs, besides talent.* She got her book bag and packed paper, pen, paste, scissors, colored pencils, and a heap of photographs of herself so that she could choose the best one.

It wasn't difficult to find an early map of Buckman at the library, but Caroline didn't know how she could find out which theater had been the very first.

"Try the vertical files," the librarian told her, and showed her where the file cabinets were that held newspaper clippings of long ago. Caroline didn't even know such files existed.

There it was at last, a brown folder marked *Theaters* on the tab. Inside was a photograph of the Cinema Theater on Main Street, which had been called the Princess Theater before that and the Royale when it first opened. And there, just as Caroline had hoped, was a newspaper story about the grand opening in 1920—the very first movie, *Pollyanna,* starring an actress named Mary Pickford!

Those old silent movies! Caroline thought. Imagine being an actress and not having to say a word because moving pictures didn't have sound back then. Everything an actress needed to tell, she did with her eyes, her lips, her hands, her posture!

Caroline studied the picture of Mary Pickford, who looked very shy, with her eyes downcast. Caroline lowered her own eyes and studied the floor.

Now terror. Silently she put her hand to her throat and shaped her mouth into a huge O, her eyes wide.

Anger next. Caroline brought her eyebrows together over the bridge of her nose. She clenched her teeth, her fists.

Sadness? She tried to think of the saddest thing that had ever happened to her, and decided it was the death of her puppy back in Ohio. Her mouth began to sag at the corners, her chin began to quiver. She could feel tears forming in her eyes.

Then she saw a boy staring at her from between the rows of books. She quickly picked up her pen and got to work.

"A Look at Yesterday and a Glimpse of Tomorrow," she had titled her story. *Nine decades ago, Mary Pickford, appearing at the old Royale Theater on Main Street, now the Cinema, took Buckman by storm,* she wrote. *And today an aspiring young actress lives in Buckman, hoping to follow in the footsteps of that famous actress. . . .*

When she had finished her story, Caroline stared again at the photo of Mary Pickford. Except for the curls, did Mary look that much different from her? she wondered. Why wasn't it possible that Caroline had been Mary Pickford in an earlier life? Why else was she so passionate about being onstage? Why else did she want to be an actress more than anything in the world?

Caroline got out the pictures of herself she had brought to use with her article. She found one the same size as the photo of Mary Pickford. Their heads in the photos were turned in the same direction. Caroline took the newspaper article over to the copy machine, put in her dime, and made a copy of the article. Back at the table, she carefully, carefully cut out Mary Pickford's shy face from the copy she had made, and slid her own photo beneath the paper so that her own face was showing through the hole.

And there she was, curls and all—Caroline Lenore Malloy Pickford. But *this* Mary Pickford was smiling.

Back she went to the copy machine and made a copy of the copy. Then another. She would not share this with anyone, of course, but it would be her dream and inspiration. When the road was rough and she was discouraged, she would get out this picture of her as Mary Pickford, and she would tell herself that anything was possible.

Finished with her article at last, Caroline put the newspaper story back in the vertical file and packed up the rest of her things. The boy who had been staring at her while she practiced her emotions peered at her over the top of a magazine, and Caroline smiled sweetly so that he would know she was perfectly normal.

■

Two days later, when Mrs. Malloy went to lunch with some of the faculty wives from the college, the three girls took their sandwiches out to eat on the grass.

It was a bit cooler than it had been for some time, and they decided to have a picnic.

"Olives," said Beth, spreading their lunch out before them. "Grapes, cupcakes . . ."

"This is a perfect day," said Caroline. "Not too hot, not too windy. If every day was like this one, summer would be my favorite season."

It was a perfect day, that is, until Eddie said, "Look!"

Caroline turned to see all four Hatford boys thundering across the bridge below.

As they came up the hill where the girls were having their picnic, Josh waved something in his hand.

"What is it?" Beth called.

"The *Old Times Tribune*," Josh said. "Their paper came out two days before ours will."

"Is it any good?" Eddie wanted to know.

"See what you think," Jake said, and Josh handed the newspaper to the girls. There on the first page was the article that had appeared in the *Buckman Bugle* ninety years before about the grand opening of the Royale Theater. The kids who had made the newspaper hadn't even bothered to rewrite the story. All they'd done was make a copy of it.

But in the photo where Mary Pickford should have been was the face of Caroline Lenore Malloy, curls and all.

Thirteen

■

Down with Tyranny!

"How the heck did the *Old Times Tribune* get this picture?" asked Jake. "You're not working for them, are you, Caroline?"

Caroline just stared.

"Caroline wasn't even born yet in 1920!" said Wally. "That can't be her."

"Duh!" said Eddie, and turned to Caroline.

Wally couldn't tell what Caroline Malloy was thinking. He knew by her face that she was just as surprised as anyone else.

Suddenly she cried, "The boy! That's who it was!"

"Huh?" said Beth.

"At the library! Some boy was watching me! I must have left a copy of that picture in the copy machine, and he took it and used it for their paper! I'll bet he was working on the *Old Times Tribune*. I'll bet he knew all along I was writing for the *Hatford Herald*."

"They probably thought they were stealing a good story," said Josh, starting to laugh. "They wanted to get it in print before we did."

"Instead, this looks ridiculous!" said Beth. "*You* look ridiculous, Caroline, with all those curls. Everyone will *know* this isn't the real Mary Pickford! Why on earth did you ever mess with her picture?"

"I . . . I just . . . just wanted to—" Caroline began, but Eddie interrupted.

"So what's the rest of their paper like?" she asked, turning the page. "Is it any good?"

"Not really," said Josh. "See for yourself. It's mostly stuff they've copied from somewhere else."

Caroline was still upset. "That picture was . . . was just a private thing that nobody else was supposed to see!" she said. And to Wally's horror, she began to cry.

The problem with Caroline's crying was that Wally couldn't tell whether it was real or fake. If actresses could cry just thinking about something, how did you know whether it was the real McCoy? They all stared at Caroline for a few seconds, waiting to see if the tears would blow over.

"Oh, it's not that bad," said Beth. "No one will know you did it. The guys doing the *Old Times Tribune* probably didn't even realize it was a fake."

Caroline's tears turned to sniffles.

"Speaking of pictures," Eddie said, "we need one

more thing to fill up our first issue, and I've got a great idea. I thought it would be fun to put all our names in one column and a baby picture of each of us in the next column. Only, they'll be all mixed up so no one can tell whose picture is whose. Readers will have to guess. And in the third issue, we'll put the right picture by the right name and people can see if they guessed right."

Caroline's face broke into a happy smile. "That's a great idea!" she said.

Oh, no! thought Wally. Eddie wasn't going to get any baby picture of him! He couldn't remember one single picture of himself as a baby that he would like to see in a newspaper. A baby with birthday cake all over his cheeks. A red-faced baby crying because he'd gotten his foot stuck in a flowerpot. A rain-soaked baby, hair plastered to his head, sitting in a puddle. A bare-bottomed baby crawling into the bathtub.

Jake and Josh felt the same way.

"Count me out," said Jake.

"Me too," said Josh. "I'm not having any baby picture in a newspaper. Not even ours."

"Oh, come on!" said Beth. "I think it's cool! It could be fun! People love to do matching games."

"Then match something else," said Jake. "Dental records. Fingerprints. You won't get any baby pictures from me."

"Well, I'm editor in chief, and you're overruled," said Eddie. "We go to press in two days, and I want a picture of each of you by tomorrow."

"I don't care if you're *commander* in chief! You can't

go bossing everyone around," said Jake. "If we don't want our baby pictures in a newspaper, then we're not going to give them to you."

"Right!" said Peter, standing up for his brothers.

For once, Wally thought, his brothers were on *his* side. Leaving the *Old Times Tribune* on the picnic blanket beside the girls, Wally and his brothers trooped back down the hill and on across the swinging bridge.

"All for one, and one for all. We stick together!" said Jake.

"Right!" Peter said again.

∎

Wally felt sure that Eddie would call again that night and say okay, the paper would go to press without the baby pictures, but she didn't.

"What if she won't put out the paper at all?" said Josh. "We're the ones who will suffer. We're the ones who need the credit."

"Her name's on those posters, remember? *The Hatford Herald, Eddie Malloy, Editor in Chief,*" said Jake. "She'll print it, don't worry. It's about time she learned that she can't do it alone."

∎

"So how's the newspaper coming along?" Mr. Hatford asked that night at dinner. He was still wearing his mail carrier's uniform, which meant he'd been working late. The fall JCPenney catalog had just come out, and when it was time to deliver those, he was always late getting home.

"Well, the first issue is supposed to come out on

Friday," Jake said. "Josh and I have done our part. The rest is up to Eddie."

"Nice going," his father said.

"I remember making a little neighborhood newspaper when I was in school," said their mother. "But I didn't have a computer then, so I wrote each copy by hand. It took forever, and I only made two of them before I gave up. I think I sold them for three cents apiece. You guys don't know how lucky you are."

"Yeah," said Wally. "Lucky us."

■

The following day Mrs. Hatford came home from the hardware store for lunch. After she'd put the tomato soup and grilled cheese sandwiches on the table, she said, "Wally, which of your baby pictures do you like best? The one of you eating your first birthday cake or the one of you sitting in a puddle?"

Wally almost choked on his cheese sandwich. "Neither one!" he yelped.

"Why are you asking?" Jake said.

"Yeah!" cried Josh. "Why do you want to know?"

Mrs. Hatford looked confused. "Well, for heaven's sake, what's the matter? Eddie called this morning before you boys were up and asked if she could have a baby picture of each of you for the newspaper. She said if I could bring them with me to work, she'd stop by the hardware store and pick them up."

"Noooooooooo!" cried the three oldest Hatford boys in unison.

"What's wrong? I wasn't going to wake you up and

ask which ones I should give her. But I just wondered which of those two pictures of Wally he liked best. I guessed the birthday cake, so that's what I gave her."

"She *tricked* us!" Josh yelled. "We told her she couldn't have any!"

"Well, how would I know that?" said his mother. "Good heavens, don't make a federal case of it. Are you and those girls fighting again? I thought you were over that by now."

"It's Eddie who's bossing us around!" said Jake. "She had no right to ask you for our pictures, and you shouldn't have given them to her without asking us."

Mrs. Hatford sighed and lowered her head. "Do you see these gray hairs?" she asked, pointing. "Do you know what's causing them?"

"Dandruff?" asked Peter.

"Boys!" said their mother. "Four boys who are driving me right out of my mind."

■

At three o'clock that afternoon, the four boys marched across the swinging bridge, up the hill to the Malloys', past the house, and on down their driveway to the road out front. Then, between the Malloys' mailbox and the lilac bush, they marched back and forth, back and forth, holding hand-lettered signs in black ink with a different message on each:

Jake held a sign that read EDDIE MALLOY, DICTATOR.

Josh's sign read INVASION OF PRIVACY.

Wally's read DOWN WITH TYRANNY!

And Peter's: WE WANT JUSTICE!

They saw Eddie, Beth, and Caroline come out on their front steps and stare at them. The UPS truck was coming down the road. It started to turn up the Malloys' drive to deliver a package, then kept going instead. Every car passing the house slowed down so that the driver could read the signs.

Half an hour later, just when Wally felt that he and his brothers were getting the hang of it, a dark green Chevy came into view and began to slow. Then it slowed even more and came to a stop.

Wally couldn't make out who was driving, but he saw the man roll his window down. Then Coach Malloy leaned out the window and said, "Hey, fellas, do you think I could go up my own driveway?"

■ ■ ■ ■ ■ ■ ■ ■ ■ ■ ■

Fourteen

■

A Roundtable Discussion

"Dad! Dad's home!" Caroline shrieked, jumping off the porch and running down the drive to meet her father.

Mr. Malloy got out of the car as his wife and daughters gathered around him.

"George!" Caroline's mother said, giving him a hug. "We didn't know you would be coming home!"

"Thought I'd surprise you and drive back for a few days. We're still negotiating that contract," Coach Malloy said. He motioned toward the end of the driveway. "Quite a welcoming committee out there, I must say."

"I can't tell what in the world is going on," Mrs. Malloy said. "It's all about the newspaper, I guess, and who is or who is not in charge. But the neighbors have been calling, wondering—"

"I'm editor in chief, so *I'm* in charge," Eddie declared. "It's a labor dispute, that's all."

"Well, I saw a 'We Want Justice!' sign down there," said her father. "I saw a 'Down with Tyranny!' sign. Sounds pretty serious to me. Not exactly the kind of thing I want in front of my house after coaching a football team all year."

"Oh, nobody will take them seriously," said Eddie.

"I don't care," said Mr. Malloy, picking up his bag. "I want you to end this. Now."

"Dad!" cried Eddie, Beth, and Caroline together.

"If I give in now, it will show I've lost control of the newspaper!" Eddie protested.

"Well? What do you think that picket line tells you? Do the honorable thing, Eddie, and take a vote," Mr. Malloy said. "And then those guys can go home." He started for the house, and Mrs. Malloy followed.

The girls looked at each other.

"That's suicide!" Beth said. "It's four against three. You *know* how the boys will vote."

"I don't care so much about using the baby pictures, though I still think it's a fun idea. It's the principle of the thing," said Eddie. "They tricked us when they named the paper. Now we should get what *we* want. They are *so* immature. There must be a way. . . ."

"Maybe if we stall long enough, they'll get tired and go home," Caroline suggested.

Mr. Malloy appeared in the doorway again. "I mean *now!*" he thundered, and Caroline knew he meant it.

"Listen," Beth said to her sisters. "There's a swing vote here. Peter's."

Eddie and Caroline began to smile.

"And you know what will change his mind," said Beth.

"Cookies!" Eddie and Caroline said together.

They walked to the end of the driveway, where the boys were parading back and forth between the mailbox and the lilac bush. Peter marched like a soldier, his back straight, his sign high over his head.

"You want to negotiate?" Eddie asked Jake.

"What's to negotiate?" Jake answered. "We don't want our baby pictures published, *period*!"

"Well, why don't you come up to the house where it's cool and we'll discuss it," Eddie told them.

The boys seemed ready for a break.

"All right. A fifteen-minute break, that's all," said Josh.

Up the driveway they went. Mr. and Mrs. Malloy were in the living room talking about the job contract back in Ohio. Eddie led the Hatford boys to the kitchen, and they all sat around the big table.

"Now, we just want to discuss this calmly like intelligent human beings," said Eddie. "A newspaper needs to please its customers, and readers enjoy things like crossword puzzles and quizzes and matching names and stuff. You know how magazines often have pictures of famous people—movie stars and basketball players—and you're supposed to match them with their high school graduation pictures?"

"We're not famous people," said Wally.

"Yet!" said Caroline.

"So if we want to please our readers, we need to lose a little pride," said Eddie. "Beth and Caroline and I are certainly ready to do *our* part. Here are three pictures of us when *we* were babies."

She went into the dining room and returned with three photos:

Eddie at eighteen months in baseball pajamas, with a much too large baseball cap all but hiding her eyes. Cute as the dickens.

Beth in an adorable pair of overalls, holding a huge storybook on her lap, bigger than she was, almost, her mouth open as though reading the book to herself. Absolutely precious.

Caroline dressed as an Easter bunny, huge ears towering over her head. Utterly charming.

"Yeah? And where are the pictures you tricked Mom into giving you?" asked Jake.

Eddie went back into the dining room and returned with four more photos. She held them up one at a time, out of the boys' reach:

Jake in a waterlogged diaper standing out under the sprinkler.

Josh sound asleep in a laundry basket, his T-shirt pulled up, showing his round belly.

Wally with both hands plunged into a birthday cake, half the frosting on his face.

And Peter staring wide-eyed at the camera, a pacifier stuck in his mouth like a cork in a bottle.

"They're cute!" Caroline insisted.

"No!" said Jake. "They're embarrassing and stupid."

"And we *don't* want you to put them in our paper," said Josh.

"I know!" said Beth. "Let's vote! But first, does anyone want some lemonade?"

"I do!" sang out Peter, swinging his legs in anticipation.

"Yeah, I'll take some," said Josh.

Eddie got down the glasses and then the ice. She poured each boy a large glass.

"Cookies?" said Beth.

"Yes!" Peter said loudly, starting to grin.

Caroline and Eddie exchanged knowing glances as Beth got the cookie canister and opened it. Her face fell. There was only one broken cookie left, and it was stale. That, and a handful of crumbs.

"Didn't Mom bake yesterday?" Beth asked in dismay.

"Apparently not," said Eddie.

Peter stared sullenly down at the piece of cookie in front of him.

"Let's vote!" said Jake impatiently. "All in favor of putting our baby pictures in the *Hatford Herald*?"

"Aye!" said Eddie, Beth, and Caroline.

"All opposed say no," said Jake.

"No!" shouted Jake and Josh and Wally and Peter, so loudly that the walls shook.

There was nothing left to do but give the photos back to the boys.

"Okay," said Eddie with a sigh. "Anybody want to stick around and help me put the paper together?"

"Sure, we'll help," said Josh.

■

When Mr. Malloy walked into the dining room later, he found Eddie at the computer in one corner, Jake and Josh taking papers out of the printer, Peter and Caroline stapling them together, Wally and Beth stacking them in piles, the whole production moving along as if on an assembly line. Anyone would have thought the kids never quarreled. Anyone would have thought that they got along like peas in a pod, grapes in a bunch, sardines in a tin.

"Now, this is what I like to see," Mr. Malloy said. "Cooperation." He smiled around the room. "When's the pub date?"

"Tomorrow," said Eddie. "We told Mr. Oldaker we'd get them to the bookstore tonight."

And Caroline asked, "How did the trip go, Dad? Are we going to move back to Ohio or not?"

"Well, I'm about seventy percent sure that we will, but there are still a number of things that bother me about the contract. I'll be driving back on Monday to see if we can work things out."

Could she stand to leave this place? Caroline wondered as she put the last newspaper in the box. Did she really want to leave this house? The river, with the swinging footbridge? The old elementary school building with the real stage and velvet curtain?

She looked across the table where Jake and Josh were

grinning at each other, smug and satisfied now that they had gotten their way. She looked at Wally, who had turned one of his pockets inside out and was intently examining the crumbs and lint and paper scraps that had fallen into his hand. At Peter, who was digging one finger up his left nostril. Well, yes and no, she decided. Maybe she wouldn't mind leaving the Hatfords at all.

Fifteen

■

Letter from Georgia

Dear Wally (and Jake and Josh and Peter):

Of course *we want to come back to Buckman, and we're not kissing any Georgia peaches, either. It's just that we signed up for a bunch of stuff here—Steve's on a diving team—so we can't leave till summer's over. Since the Malloys aren't sure whether they're moving back to Ohio or not, Mom said we should keep our house here till September. That will give them time to find another place if they stay. Dad will be back August first, though, so he can start training the football team.*

How does our house look? The girls haven't changed anything, have they? Boy, they better not do anything to our rooms! We don't trust those Malloy girls any more than you do.

Yeah, I'm sorry we couldn't be in on that newspaper thing. I think I would have liked doing it even if you didn't. I wouldn't want Eddie Malloy bossing me around, though. I hope it turns out to be the best newspaper of all.

I hope everyone in Buckman reads it! I hope the Malloys go back to Ohio for good, and that when we get back from Georgia, everything will be just like it always was.
Bill (and Danny and Steve and Tony and Doug)

P.S. If you want to be scared out of your socks, your underwear, and the hair on your head, get that old video Invasion of the Body Snatchers. *You won't sleep for a week after that.*

Sixteen

■

Uh-oh

Copies of the *Hatford Herald* were neatly stacked by the window of Oldakers' Bookstore, all four pages of it, stapled together.

It was exciting to see the newspaper there on the window shelf between the *Buckman Bugle* and the *New York Times*. Beth took a picture of it, and Mike Oldaker let Peter stand at the door for a while, handing a copy to each customer who left the store. Both Mrs. Malloy and Mrs. Hatford asked for extra copies to send to relatives.

There was an editorial by Eddie saying that the newspaper was a summer reading project for students entering the seventh grade and would be about some of the historic happenings in Buckman. Then she named both her sisters as well as herself and all the Hatford boys as being on the newspaper staff.

The rest of the first page was an early map of Buckman, before many of the new developments and streets had been built. It showed every spot where there had been a swinging bridge crossing the river, and pointed out some of the buildings downtown—Ethel's Bakery, Oldakers' Bookstore, a cobbler's shop, and the old Royale Theater, now called the Cinema.

The second page of the paper had an article by Eddie on the swinging bridges, and Jake's write-up of an old college football game. There was a comic strip by Josh on the ways people used to keep cool before air-conditioning, as well as a boxed news item at the bottom of the page:

> The *Hatford Herald* wishes to point out to the *Old Times Tribune* that the photograph in their first issue was not of Mary Pickford, the actress, as stated, but none other than Buckman's own Caroline Lenore Malloy, who hopes someday to appear on Broadway. Miss Malloy wishes to thank the *Old Times Tribune* for comparing her so favorably to that famous actress.

"Oh, Eddie, that's perfect!" Caroline said. "That'll fix their wagon!" The downside was that Eddie wouldn't let her write an article about herself as an aspiring actress, now that this piece had appeared in a rival paper, but a little publicity was better than no publicity at all.

Caroline's story about Bessie and Tessie Crane took up the whole third page. She had neglected to get a photo of the two sisters for her article, but she put in almost every word of what she had been told—how bossy Tessie had been, how jealous of her sister, how they got along well in public but fought like cats and dogs at home. Caroline was glad that the elderly woman had said at least *some* good things about her sister, but they weren't much. It would certainly make for juicy reading, Eddie had said, laughing, when they printed it up. She had chosen a good title for it too: *"Memories of a Beloved but Bossy Sister."*

This would probably get the most attention of all, Caroline thought smugly. Everyone liked to read gossip, and one sister's saying that their relationship was not what it seemed would be the talk of the town.

With Coach Malloy home for the weekend, Mrs. Malloy invited the Hatford family over for dinner that evening to celebrate the first issue of the *Hatford Herald*.

"It's a beautiful day, and I thought I would set up two tables under the beech tree and we could eat outside," she said.

"Sounds like a good idea," said her husband.

At six o'clock, the Hatfords came across the footbridge below, all six of them, in shorts and T-shirts, bringing along some folding chairs and a caramel cake.

"Nice of you to have us over!" Mr. Hatford said, helping himself to the pickled beets. "Best day for a picnic we've had all summer. I sure hate the thought of your leaving Buckman, George."

"Well, it's seventy percent certain we're going back,

but we've really enjoyed our stay here," Coach Malloy said. "There will be a lot to miss."

"Wonderful cake, Ellen," said Mrs. Malloy.

"My mother's recipe," Mrs. Hatford said.

When the meal was over and Wally had eaten two pieces of cake, he and Caroline lay on their backs on the other side of the beech tree, looking up into the leaves. Wally was watching a caterpillar dangling from a thin strand of silk, blowing back and forth in the evening breeze.

For her part, Caroline was trying her best to be Wally for the moment—to see the world through his eyes.

"Guess how much a rope of spider's silk, one inch thick, would hold," Wally was saying to her.

"I don't know," said Caroline.

"Seventy-four tons," said Wally. "I read it in a science book."

"No kidding," said Caroline.

"And you know what else?" said Wally. "It would be three times as strong as a one-inch rope made of iron."

"Amazing," said Caroline. What was even more amazing was that Wally Hatford could be perfectly happy—would be *happiest,* in fact—if he could just spend the whole summer quietly studying stuff like this: spiderwebs and anthills. That he was most miserable when he had to get up in front of people and perform.

How strange and interesting it was that she was just the opposite. If Caroline did not have people watching her and applauding, if she was not the center of attention, she felt she would shrivel up. How wonderful that there were people who loved to perform and people who loved to watch.

She was squinting now as she studied the caterpillar, because her booklet on auras said that all living things had an energy force around them, even something as small as a caterpillar. She wondered what color a caterpillar's energy force would be. Yellow, she imagined. Maybe she did see a little something around it—sort of a mist, maybe.

What she heard, however, was the sound of a car grinding slowly up the driveway. Jake and Josh and Eddie and Beth stopped their croquet game up by the house, and everyone turned to see an ancient Oldsmobile moving at five miles per hour toward the clearing between the house and garage.

"Looks as though you have company," Mr. Hatford said.

The car came to a stop, the door on the driver's side opened, and a little old lady stepped out, leaning on her cane.

Caroline sat up. "Why, it's Bessie Crane!" she said.

The elderly woman glared at Caroline. "It is *not*!" she said sharply, her voice carrying all the way across the lawn. "It's *Tessie,* for your information, and your newspaper made it sound as though it was my sister talking about *me*!"

"What?" cried Caroline.

"Uh-oh," Mr. Hatford said under his breath.

"You got our names mixed up!" the woman said indignantly, and she shook her cane at Caroline. "You've got me dead and in the ground, young lady, and Bessie saying all sorts of evil things about me. And you call yourself a reporter!"

Eddie gasped and hurried over.

"We are so sorry, ma'am," she said. "It was a terrible mistake, and we'll put a retraction in the next issue."

"Retraction, resmaction!" Tessie Crane scoffed. "The damage is done! Now folks think it was *me* who died, and some of them are even saying 'Good riddance.'"

"Ms. Crane, please sit down and have some dessert with us," Mrs. Malloy said, giving a quick, furious glance at Caroline. "Mrs. Hatford has baked the most delicious caramel cake, and you really must try it."

Humphing and scowling, Ms. Crane turned to look at the seven-layer cake. "Caramel, eh?" she said, and shook her head; but then she studied it some more. "That's no ready-made frosting, I can tell."

"Indeed it's not," said Mrs. Hatford. "My mother wouldn't have thought of doing such a thing!"

Immediately a folding chair was moved closer to the old woman, a saucer and fork were produced, and when Tessie Crane had sat down and placed her cane on the ground, Mrs. Malloy went back inside to get her a cup of tea.

"Oh, I do remember your sister," Mr. Hatford said. "I used to deliver mail to that side of town, you know. I still remember how Bessie would meet me at the door some days, and she'd say, 'Tom, if you can't bring me anything but bills, don't bring me anything at all.' "

Everyone laughed then, even Ms. Crane.

"That was just like her too!" she said, taking a second bite of cake and letting the frosting roll around on her tongue. "She'd put those bills on *my* side of the desk, and guess who she expected to pay them!"

"If you'd loan us your favorite photograph, we'd like to put it in the next issue of the *Hatford Herald* with our apology for our mistake," Eddie said.

"Hmmm," said Ms. Crane, licking her fork to make sure she got every last bit of the sugary stuff. "I always did like that picture of me in my flowered dress. . . . Yes, I think I'll loan you that one, and you can let your readers know that I'm very much alive indeed." Then she turned to Mr. Hatford again:

"And *I* remember your *father*!" she said. "He was an anthropologist there at the college, wasn't he?"

"Yes, he was," said Mr. Hatford. "It's nice to know he's remembered."

Tessie Crane began to smile again. "Well, Bessie and I thought he was about the handsomest man in Buckman, that's why we remembered him. But of course he was already married to your mother."

The grown-ups were talking memories now, and Caroline thought it was a good time to slip away. She wanted to put a copy of the first issue of the newspaper in her scrapbook. She wanted to admire her byline there on the third page, and never mind her mistake. It was a shame that reporters couldn't get their pictures on the page beside their stories.

She had scarcely reached the kitchen before Eddie followed her in. "How could you make such a dumb mistake, Caroline?" Eddie scolded. "We could get *sued* over mistakes like that!"

"Tessie . . . Bessie . . . they sound too much alike, Eddie!" Caroline said plaintively. "*She* certainly didn't mind saying all those bad things about her sister!"

"Well, get your facts straight! That's what newspapers are supposed to do! The next time you go on assignment, check and double-check. Don't mess up!" Eddie told her.

Caroline saluted and clicked her heels together. "Yes, *sir*!" she barked, but nothing could ruin her pleasure in knowing that *her* story was probably going to be the best-read article in the whole paper.

■ ■ ■ ■ ■ ■ ■ ■ ■ ■ ■

Seventeen

■

In the Dark

The book that had bothered Wally at the start of July, *A Ghost's Revenge,* was under his bed. He hadn't known it was there until he got an overdue notice in the mail.

He should have taken the book back to the library right then, but he didn't. He should never have opened the book again, but he did. The story he wanted so much to forget—the story about the ghostly presence that stayed behind to haunt—was so real that he could almost believe it.

It wasn't the kind of story where a misty figure floats into your room at night and says "Boo!" It was the kind where things happened that couldn't be explained. Sounds. Touch. Cold. Without the writer's saying so, you just knew by the feeling of cold and dread that the ghost was in the room. Everything in Wally's room seemed to move when he wasn't looking.

"This is nuts," Wally kept telling himself. "This never happened. It's only a story. It's all made up." Nonetheless, those words—those simple black marks on white paper—turned his skin to gooseflesh.

So instead of taking *A Ghost's Revenge* back to the library, Wally read it again to see if this time he could laugh about it. He couldn't. In fact, it scared him more the second time around.

The part that bothered him most was when the man first knew the ghost was there. He had heard a scratching, scraping, clawing sound in his cellar. *Exactly* the kind of scratching, scraping, clawing sound that Wally had heard down at Oldakers'. If you didn't have good ears, you might not have heard it at all. Wally Hatford had good ears.

The next night, the story went, the scratching, scraping, clawing sound came from the man's first-floor library, and the night after that, it was on the stairs. The night after that, it was in the man's bedroom, and then it was beside his bed. Wally knew that if he ever woke up in the night to hear a scratching, scraping, clawing sound in his closet, he'd probably die of a heart attack.

Twice he had called Mike Oldaker to remind him that there would be only two more issues of the *Hatford Herald.* There were only two more weeks for Wally to get the scoop that even the *Buckman Bugle* wouldn't get till later. But both times Mike had told him, "Not yet, Wally, not yet."

The more Wally thought about it, the more worried

he was that it was all a trick. The more he played over in his mind those sounds down in the cellar of Oldakers' Bookstore, the more he worried it was a secret that shouldn't be kept.

He had made up his mind, however. That night after dark, after the bookstore closed, he was going to stand outside and peer through the window. He was going to wait and see if anything came up out of the trapdoor in the hardwood floor, right there near the cashier's counter. If a beast of some sort was down there, it had to be fed, didn't it? *Some*one had to tend to it when no one was looking. And if it was a ghost, a trapdoor wouldn't hold it in. Wally had to know. He wasn't going to settle for being scared the rest of his life.

On this particular evening, his mother was working late at the hardware store and his dad had taken Jake and Josh and Peter bowling.

"Sure you don't want to come, Wally?" his dad had called.

"Nope," said Wally.

He did not like to bowl. "Old Gutter Ball Wally," Jake called him, because—more often than not—the ball rolled into the gutter without hitting any pins at all.

Wally couldn't understand the attraction. Why would you want to spend an entire evening trying to knock down some pins? If that was so important to you, why not just walk to the end of the alley and kick them over with your foot? What was the point? What did you learn? He would far rather lie under a beech tree and watch a caterpillar dangle from a strand of silk.

But tonight it wasn't a caterpillar he was going to watch for. It was something that scratched. Something that scraped. Something that thumped occasionally and clawed, and for all Wally knew, moaned when no one could hear it. Maybe even rattled its chains!

As soon as dusk settled in, as soon as Wally was sure that the bookstore had closed for the night, he put on a dark long-sleeved T-shirt and dark jeans and went outside, down College Avenue toward town. Never mind the heat; Wally wanted to be as invisible as he possibly could.

The streets were almost deserted now as, one after another, the stores began to close and lights went off in shop windows. Wally moved quickly along the sidewalk, hands in his pockets. He passed Ethel's Bakery and the linen store, glad that the hardware store where his mother worked was on the far side of town, and that the bowling alley where his dad and brothers had gone was a mile in the other direction.

Mike Oldaker had just come out of his bookstore and was locking up. From a doorway two stores down, Wally watched him pause with his key still in his hand. He seemed to be thinking of something else. Then he unlocked the door again and went back inside.

Wally crept forward until he got to the display window. He cupped his hands around his eyes and peered hard through the glass. He saw Mr. Oldaker bending over the trapdoor. He saw him *lift* the trapdoor. A square of light shone up out of the darkness for only a few seconds. Then, while Wally watched, Mr. Oldaker closed the door again.

Wally slipped back to his hiding place and stayed until Mike Oldaker had come out and left for good. Then Wally crept back to the doorway of the bookstore and waited.

The sky grew darker still. A breeze blew down Main Street, whipping up stray pages of newspapers, blowing them this way and that until they caught against a step or a lamppost. The linen store's light went out. The owner of the thrift shop locked her door and went home. Even the light in Larkin's Pharmacy went out.

Every few minutes, perspiring in his long-sleeved shirt, Wally turned around to face the window in the bookstore, cup his hands around his eyes, and peer inside. He could just make out a thin line of light coming around all four edges of the trapdoor.

If people weren't looking for it, if they didn't know that the trapdoor was there, they could walk right by the store and not give it a second look.

There *was* something down there. Something that needed light. What if Mike Oldaker was creating a monster in the cellar of his bookstore? He was a smart man. He read lots of books. What if he was making a Frankenstein's monster? What if there was a horrible beast chained to a table down under the floor?

Goose bumps rose up on Wally's arms. It wasn't just bones, as Mike had said. It was something alive!

Half an hour went by. An hour. A police car moved slowly down the street. If an officer saw a boy standing in the doorway of a closed shop, he would surely stop. Wally flattened himself against the side of the doorway and turned his face away from the street. The policeman must not have seen him, because the cruiser went on toward the corner.

When Wally stepped out and looked in the bookstore window again, he saw that the thin lines of light in the floor had gone out. He pressed his face even closer to the glass. The store was dark, lit only by a dim night-light near the cash register. Wally could just make out the counters, the book racks.

And then, while he stood there still as a stone, the trapdoor opened—an inch . . . two inches. . . . Someone—or something—was pushing it open from underneath. Wally could barely see the hand that held it.

And suddenly, as quickly as the trapdoor had opened, it closed. There was no light at all around the edges. The someone—or something—must have seen Wally out there peering through the window and ducked back inside. Someone—or something—didn't want Wally Hatford to know it was down there. Wally made a beeline for home.

He ran into his house and locked the door behind him. He ran up to his room and closed that door as well. He turned on every light, including the light in his closet, and sat against the headboard of his bed, holding a pillow close to his chest.

How did you decide when you shouldn't keep a

secret any longer? he wondered. When should you at least tell your mom and dad? What if there was a creature that crawled out at night and did horrible things before it returned to its hiding place in Oldakers' cellar?

If I hear of anyone being murdered, I'll tell, Wally decided. But that would be too late. *If I hear of anyone getting beaten up, I'll tell,* he thought. Then, *If I even hear of a cat or dog being hurt, I'll tell.* And finally, *If I hear of anybody or anything mysteriously missing, that's when I'll tell my folks.*

Downstairs there was a click. Wally stiffened, straining to hear. The soft shutting of a door. Silence. He swallowed, his heart pounding hard under his shirt.

Then there were faint footsteps on the floor below. Then creaking noises on the stairs. Wally clutched the pillow even more tightly.

His doorknob began to turn. The door began to open.

"Yaaaaaaah!" Wally cried out in terror.

Mrs. Hatford entered the room. "Wally, what on earth? I thought you were going bowling with your dad!"

"I didn't want to go," said Wally.

"So I see."

"I decided to just stay home."

"Uh-huh," said his mother.

"I decided I don't like to bowl that much."

"So you'd rather stay home with a pillow over your stomach?" Mrs. Hatford crossed the floor and went over to the bed, studying him. "Are you sick?" she asked.

"Nope," said Wally.

"You can tell me anything. You know that, don't you?" she said.

"Yep," said Wally.

"Do you want to talk?" she asked.

"Nope," said Wally.

"Well, if you change your mind, I'm downstairs," she said, and went out.

"Okay," said Wally. And just knowing he *could* tell her if he wanted made him feel a little better. But he got up and pulled down his blinds, just in case.

Eighteen

■

Haunted House

The second issue of the *Hatford Herald* was almost ready to roll. Beth's photo of the haunted house wasn't as good as she had hoped, but if the sky had been brighter, the house wouldn't have looked so spooky.

"You've got exactly an hour to finish your story," Eddie told her. "I've got to know how much space to allow on the second page."

"I'm hurrying! I'm hurrying!" Beth said, typing as fast as she could. "I found out some more about it at the library. There's a picture of it in a book called *Historic Houses of Buckman,* and it says it was designed by a local architect who did seven other houses here."

"Are you just copying things out of that book then, or what?" asked Eddie. "We need to be original, you know."

"No, I'm writing a whole story," said Beth. "This is

the only one of those eight houses still standing. And I can say that in *this* house, someone really did see a ghost."

Of course there had to be a retraction on the first page about Tessie Crane's untimely death—no death at all, in fact. *The* Hatford Herald *wishes to report that Ms. Tessie Crane is not deceased in the least,* Eddie had written, *and that the reporter, Caroline Malloy, was in error when she mixed up the sisters. She is sorry for any inconvenience this may have caused.*

Jake had turned in a story about a high school baseball game in 1964, Josh had drawn a comic strip about the first cars to appear on Main Street, and Caroline's story about the man who had fought in World War I was ready to go. Eddie herself had researched how much things had cost in years gone by, comparing them with what they cost now, and even Mrs. Malloy found that story interesting.

"Bread cost only two cents a loaf back in 1903?" she said. "And look! You could buy a whole house for a little over three thousand dollars!"

"Check out the cars, Mom. I didn't even know they *had* cars in 1903. You could buy a Cadillac for seven hundred and fifty dollars!" Eddie said.

Caroline, looking over her mother's shoulder, laughed. "Without a top, of course. Thirty dollars extra if you want a roof!"

"This is fascinating," Mrs. Malloy said. "I think your readers are really going to enjoy this. Let's send a copy to your dad."

At last Beth finished her story. "Done!" she said, exchanging places with Eddie at the computer. Eddie, in turn, would put the copy into columns, just like in a regular newspaper. Beth's story began:

> A forlorn old house sits waiting at the corner of Hazel and Bennington Streets, but no one knows, waiting for what? It's as though the family living there suddenly fled, leaving everything just the way it was—a saucepan on the stove, a shoe by the couch, a jacket thrown over a chair.
>
> "I have never seen anyone go in or out," said a neighbor. "I've never seen a light on in a window."
>
> The yard is mostly bare, and what grass there is has not been mowed. But one terrified Buckman resident claims to have seen the ghastly image of a ghostly girl looking out a darkened window.
>
> "I fled in terror," said this person, who asked that her name not be revealed. "I know what I saw, and I am not making this up."
>
> Things may be peaceful during the day, but at night, who knows what lurks in deserted houses? Who knows what walks those dusty floors? Who knows . . . ?

■

While her sisters worked on the newspaper, Caroline curled up on a wicker couch on the front porch. The day was warm, the breeze gentle, the cushions inviting, and Caroline's eyes began to close.

Once she had fallen asleep on this warm afternoon,

it was hard to wake up. Drifting in and out of dreams, she was conscious of voices inside the house, footsteps now and then, or cars passing on the road. But her arms and legs felt like noodles, limp and lifeless, and it was so pleasant on the porch that she had the energy only to breathe.

She was dreaming about the day she had tried to make herself look like the actress Shirley Temple—the curly hair, the dimpled cheeks, the necklace, the smile . . .

And then, before she had even moved an inch, Caroline remembered something else. Every muscle in her body tensed. Every nerve in her scalp went on alert. The ghastly image of the ghostly girl she had seen in the window of the haunted house had been wearing that same necklace! That could only mean one thing: that what Caroline had seen in the window that evening at the haunted house, the image that had startled her so, was her own reflection. She had screamed and run at the sight of *herself*!

There had been no ghost! There had been no girl! Caroline bolted up, swinging her legs off the couch. She had to stop the presses!

"Eddie?" she called.

When Caroline rushed indoors, Mrs. Malloy was using her portable sewing machine on one side of the dining room table.

"She's gone, Caroline. Wally came over to pick up the newspapers, and she and Beth helped carry them over to the bookstore.

III

"They went to Oldakers'?" Caroline gasped. "You mean the paper's out?"

"Sweetheart, you've been asleep!" her mother said. "Didn't you hear Eddie ask if you wanted to go with them? They left about an hour ago. They probably stopped somewhere for ice cream on the way back."

Caroline went up to her room and lay facedown on her bed. *You have to get your facts straight!* Eddie had scolded her when she made the mistake about Tessie Crane. *Check and double-check!* Now it was Beth who would be in big trouble. She had listened to Caroline and written what she'd said, and it was all Caroline's fault.

Sooner or later she was going to have to tell Eddie and Beth and the whole Hatford tribe that she had seen no ghost. After that, she'd have to explain it to everyone. If anyone could see her aura now, it would be black, black, black, she was sure.

■

At dinner that evening, all Caroline could think about was leaving town. "If we move back to Ohio, how soon can we leave?" she asked.

"We're not leaving until we've given our tenants thirty days' notice," Mrs. Malloy said. "We rented out our house to another family, remember?"

"Then if Dad stays in Ohio by himself all during August, where will he live till we get our house back?" Caroline asked.

"He'll rent an apartment for a month," said her mother.

"Maybe I should go cook for him," said Caroline.

"What?" said Mrs. Malloy.

"And do his laundry," said Caroline.

Her sisters laughed. "Caroline, you've got two pairs of socks and some underwear on the bathroom floor that have been there for three days, not to mention your towel," said Beth. "You don't even take care of your own laundry."

"Besides, you always wanted to be famous, didn't you?" said Eddie. "When people read Beth's article about the haunted house, they'll want to talk to the person who saw the ghastly ghost of a girl in the window, and all sorts of people will be calling."

"I won't be famous," said Caroline plaintively. "I'll be *infamous,* Eddie!" Her chin began to tremble. "I've done a terrible and awful thing."

Mrs. Malloy stopped eating. "*What* terrible and awful thing, Caroline?" And when Caroline didn't answer, she said more sternly, "Caroline, *now* what have you done?"

"I thought I saw the ghost of a girl in the window, Mother, but it was only me. My reflection. I just realized."

"How do you know it was you?" asked her mother.

"Because I just remembered she was wearing my necklace."

"Oh, Caroline, for Pete's sake!" said Eddie. "The paper's already been printed. People are picking up copies at Oldakers' this very minute!"

"I know! I know!" Caroline said miserably.

As though that weren't enough to ruin their dinner, the phone rang just then. Wanting desperately to escape her sisters' anger, Caroline pushed away from the table and ran to answer. It was Mr. Hatford.

"Caroline," he said. "About that house over on Hazel Street, it belongs to the Parker family. They're on a six-month trip to Europe, and I've been forwarding their mail. I don't think they're going to be very happy when they get back and discover that the *Hatford Herald* said their house is haunted."

Nineteen

■

Bones!

"**M**aybe we should quit while we can," Jake said sullenly as the four Hatford boys and the three Malloy girls gathered on the Hatfords' front steps. "Beth, you know those neighbors who said they'd never seen anyone go in or out? Who never saw lights in the windows?"

"They *did* tell me that!" Beth insisted.

"Well, Dad says they've only lived there a month. Of *course* they've never seen anyone go in or out! Of *course* they never saw any lights in the windows! They never even knew the Parkers. They never knew they were in Europe."

Beth moaned and sank down even lower on the step. Caroline saw Eddie close her eyes in dismay.

"Sometimes you need more than facts!" said Josh. "You have to use your head. Dad's mad at us because the sheriff feels he has to send out a car every so often to keep an eye on that house, now that we've announced to the world it's been abandoned."

"Buckman isn't exactly the world," Eddie put in.

"And anyone can see that with newspapers and leaves blowing all around the yard, no one's there to take care of it," Caroline said, trying to defend her sisters. "A burglar would have figured that out by now. He didn't need to read it in our newspaper."

"We'll make up for it," Eddie said quickly. "We'll make the last issue of our newspaper so spectacular that everyone will forgive us for this and the Tessie-Bessie mix-up."

"Yeah? What do you suggest?" said Josh.

Nobody had an answer. About all they had left for the final issue was the story of Sara Phillips's aunt Irene and her quilts. Who would buy a newspaper just for that? Wally's mind raced ahead to the creature in the Oldakers' cellar. Mike Oldaker simply *had* to come through with that scoop. Wally had almost decided that if Mike hadn't kept his promise by the time the third issue came out, he would write a story about the noises coming from the cellar, and *then* wouldn't Mike Oldaker be sorry!

"Has anybody been murdered lately?" Wally asked softly.

The others turned, staring at him.

"I mean, has anybody been bitten or attacked, or are any pets missing?" Wally added.

"What are you talking about?" said Jake. "Even if

there were, we wouldn't be the ones to report it. This is supposed to be historical. We're not writing about what's happening around here now. Everything we write has to be about old stuff."

"I know!" said Peter brightly. "We could write about Grandpa!"

"What *about* Grandpa?" asked Wally.

"*He* was old."

"So?" said Jake.

"And he liked to study old things," said Peter.

Peter was right, Wally thought. Grandpa Hatford studied people of long ago. But *everybody* had a grandpa who did *some*thing. Why not write about *anybody*'s grandpa?

"Yeah. Right," said Jake. "Okay, Peter. You and Wally write a story about Grandpa."

"Hey! C'mon!" Wally protested.

"All you've done so far is take copy back and forth between our houses and carry newspapers down to Oldakers'," said Josh. "It wouldn't hurt you to write something."

But Wally didn't want to write. He liked to spell, but he didn't especially like to write. "*I'm* not getting any credit toward summer reading!" he said.

"Well, do a good job with your story and we'll put it on the front page," said Jake.

■

Embarrassing, that's what it was.

Grandpa was an anthropologist, Wally wrote. *He had a cupboard full of pottery pieces and shells and stuff. He could tell you a lot about people he had never met because they lived a long time ago, but he couldn't tell you much about his neighbors.*

That was about all Wally could think of to say, and he'd only gotten that far because that's what he'd heard his dad say. Grandpa Hatford had died when Wally was five, so he didn't remember much about him.

"Come *on,* Peter! Quit fooling around and help!" Wally said irritably as Peter ran his Matchbox cars along the window ledge, making a fearful racket when they crashed and fell to the floor.

Peter dutifully put the cars aside and walked over. "What do you want me to do?"

"Remember something about Grandpa. Any stories at all about him," said Wally.

"I only remember his pictures!" said Peter. "He was tall and had a mustache."

"Thanks a lot."

"And he had big hands and big ears."

"Yeah," said Wally, remembering now. "And he always had an arrowhead or something in his pocket to show us."

There were only two days left before the last issue of the *Hatford Herald* would be published. The *Old Times Tribune,* of course, came out with the story about how the "abandoned" house the *Hatford Herald* had written about wasn't abandoned at all. Wally couldn't wait till this whole project was over. Then he would have one full month left of summer to do whatever he wanted. It would *not* be anything to do with the Malloys. It would not have anything to do with girls at all. It wouldn't even have anything to do with his brothers. Maybe he would just crawl up in a tree and stay there. Study the leaves and the stars.

The following night after dinner, however, something happened. The phone rang, and because Wally was finishing up kitchen duty, he answered.

"Wally?" came a man's voice. "This is Mike. Mike Oldaker. I want you to round up all the kids who are working on your newspaper, tell them you've got a big scoop, and come over to the bookstore right away."

"Now?"

"As soon as you can get here. But don't tell anyone else. Just come." And Mike hung up.

Wally stood holding the phone in one hand, the dish towel in the other. Then he put down the towel and called the Malloys. Eddie answered.

"Big scoop. Top secret. Meet us at Oldakers' as soon as you can get there," he said, and hung up, just as Mike had done.

Wally ran upstairs, where Jake and Josh were typing up a story on their computer. "Big scoop!" he said breathlessly. "Top secret. Mike Oldaker called. He wants us to come to the bookstore right away and not tell anyone. He'll give us a story for our newspaper!"

"Wow!" said Jake, leaping to his feet, his eyes wide.

The boys tore downstairs.

"We're going to the bookstore, Mom," Josh called.

"Are you taking Peter?" Mrs. Hatford called back.

"Yeah. C'mon, Peter," said Wally, and all four boys charged out the door.

"What *is* it? What did he say?" asked Jake.

"I can't tell you," said Wally.

"What do you mean, you can't tell us?" asked Josh.

"My lips are sealed," said Wally.

"Oh, come on, Wally!" said Jake, punching his arm.

"You can torture me, pull out all my fingernails, but I still won't tell," Wally insisted, not mentioning, of course, that he didn't know much more than they did. Except for those noises. And the light coming from under the trapdoor.

His heart pounded inside his chest. He hoped it wasn't a trick. He imagined Mike Oldaker opening the trapdoor and a hand reaching out and grabbing Wally's leg. He imagined the trapdoor opening and a huge life force sucking them down into a black hole.

But now they were racing down College Avenue. Now they were turning onto Main Street. Now they were running up the sidewalk to the bookstore, with its CLOSED sign on the door, the Malloy girls at their heels.

Mike was waiting for them inside. So was a man with glasses, and dirt on the knees of his pants.

"Hello," said Mike, letting them in and locking the door behind them. Wally looked around uneasily. So did Caroline, her eyes huge.

"I want you to meet a friend of mine, Gordon Rawley, who's working on his PhD from Morgan State University, where your grandfather, Wally, got his degree," Mike said.

The big man named Gordon reached out and shook Wally's hand while the others stared. The skin on Gordon's hand was rough, Wally discovered. And the fingernails were dirty.

"It was something your grandfather wrote in *his* thesis that gave Gordon the idea that there might be the remains of an ancient settlement right here in Upshur County," said Mike.

"What kind of settlement?" asked Eddie.

Mr. Rawley said, "We call them the Archaic people. We knew they lived in the northern and eastern pan-handles between 7000 and 1000 BC, but your grand-father seemed to think they might also have had a settlement where Buckman is today. In fact, right under our downtown."

Wally's eyes opened so wide he thought they might push his eyebrows right off the top of his head. Maybe the bookstore *was* haunted. Maybe it was haunted by people of long ago!

"And because this bookstore is the only building left on the block with a dirt floor in its cellar, Gordon asked if he could do some digging down there in secret to see if he could find anything," Mike explained.

"And I did!" said Mr. Rawley, smiling. "Bones. Pieces of bones, anyway. A few shards of pottery." He reached into his pocket and carefully drew out a few fragments.

"Wow!" said Jake.

"But why did you have to keep it secret?" asked Wally.

"Because there are a couple of guys in my department

at the university who got wind of my idea, and my thesis will be a lot more important if I'm the first one to discover these artifacts in Buckman," Mr. Rawley explained.

"Well, I haven't told anyone," said Wally, as his brothers gasped and the girls gaped.

"That's good," said Mr. Rawley. "I'm just lucky enough to be friends with Mike here, and I remembered this cellar. He and I used to play down there sometimes when we were kids, back when his dad ran the store, but we had no idea that there might be something historic about it."

"Wally knew about this all the time?" Jake exclaimed.

Mike grinned. "He knew there was something secret going on in our cellar, but he didn't know what."

"So can we break the story in the *Hatford Herald*?" asked Josh excitedly.

"Absolutely," said Mike. "Gordon has written an article for this Sunday's *Buckman Bugle,* but since it was your grandfather who's really responsible for this, we thought you guys should be the first to spill the beans. I tipped off Wally a few weeks ago, and he promised he'd keep it secret."

Jake and Josh turned to grin at Wally. So did the Malloys.

"Hey, Wally, nice going!" said Jake, punching his arm again.

"All this time he's been sitting on a scoop!" said Eddie.

Wally was the center of attention, and he actually found himself smiling. He had goose bumps on his arms, but not because he was scared. Maybe he *wouldn't* want to sit in a tree all summer long with no one else to talk to. Maybe sometimes it *was* sort of nice to do something different, even with people as weird as the Malloys.

■

Two days later when the *Hatford Herald* came out, the banner headline read *News Flash . . . Important Discovery!* Wally, with the help of Jake and Josh, had written the story of the discovery in the cellar of Oldakers' Bookstore.

All afternoon and evening the phone rang. Friends and neighbors congratulated the boys on a top story, and the *Buckman Bugle* wanted a picture of the four Hatford boys standing in front of the bookstore to use in its Sunday edition, along with Gordon Rawley's article.

When Sunday came and their picture appeared, Wally had to tell people again and again the story of how Mike Oldaker had told him there were bones down there in the bookstore's cellar, and Wally hadn't known whether they were the bones of someone dead or alive. He talked about the scratching and scraping and clawing and thumping, at which point Peter, who never tired of the story, provided the sound effects.

■

Jake and Josh and Wally and Peter, along with Eddie, Beth, and Caroline, walked downtown to pick up the copy of the *Hatford Herald* that Mrs. Hatford had taken to a frame shop. They were going to present the framed newspaper to Oldakers' Bookstore to hang on the wall in appreciation for Mike's letting them have the biggest scoop of the year.

What a day! They still didn't know whether the girls were moving back to Ohio or staying in Buckman, but they weren't thinking about that now. They were thinking about the triple scoops of ice cream they were going to have later at the soda fountain in Larkin's drugstore—a great way to celebrate the final issue of their newspaper.

"All ready to go!" the man at the frame shop said. He picked up a large rectangular package wrapped in brown paper. "I taped it up good so you wouldn't get fingerprints on the glass," he explained. "Now see if you can get it down to the bookstore all in one piece."

"Thanks!" Jake grinned. "We'll take good care of it."

So down the street they went, Wally in the lead.

"What's this?" said Mike, looking up from the cash register as the group entered the store.

"A token of our appreciation, so that no matter where we go or what we do in life, you will always remember us as—"

"Stuff it, Caroline," said Eddie.

"It's just something we'd like you to hang in your store," said Wally.

"Well, this is a surprise!" said Mike. He took off the wrapper and stared at the last copy of the *Hatford Herald*. "This is great!" he said. "This is really neat!" He looked around at the walls of his bookstore. "There's a spot by the front door next to the window. Why don't we hang it there?"

"Sounds good to us!" said Eddie.

A clerk appeared with a hammer and nail, and after Mike had hung the framed newspaper, the Malloys and the Hatfords stood back to make sure it was straight.

"A little to the left," said Josh.

"Now a little to the right," said Caroline.

Finally it seemed balanced perfectly, and they all gathered around to admire it.

"Hey!" Eddie said suddenly. "What's that?"

"What?" asked Beth.

"There at the bottom!" said Eddie. "Don't you see it?" She pointed.

At the very bottom of the front page, in a box insert, someone had added these words:

> This is the last issue of our paper, the *Hatford Herald*. We have enjoyed bringing you stories of Buckman in the olden days and hope you enjoyed it too. The boys—Peter, Wally, Jake, and Josh Hatford—who wrote the important stuff. The girls—Caroline, Beth, and Eddie Malloy—who wrote the rest.
>
> **BOYS ROCK!**

■ ■ ■ ■ ■ ■ ■ ■ ■ ■ ■ ■ ■

About the Author

Phyllis Reynolds Naylor writes:

"I don't remember starting a neighborhood newspaper when I was young, but I did write little books. We didn't have much money, so I was only allowed to use scrap paper that was blank on one side. I was the author, the illustrator, and the binder, all three. When a book was finished, I would cut an envelope in two, paste half of it in the front of the book, and stick an index card in it like the card in a library book. Then I would sign it out to neighborhood children and charge a penny if it was returned overdue! My mother saved many of these books, and I take some of them with me when I speak at a school. What did I write about? Well, one of them is called 'The Food Fairies,' and it's about all the food in a refrigerator going to war. I even drew a picture of the hot dogs with rifles over their shoulders. It wouldn't win any prizes, believe me."

Phyllis Reynolds Naylor is the author of more than 125 books, including the Newbery Award–winning *Shiloh* and the other two books in the Shiloh trilogy, *Shiloh Season* and *Saving Shiloh*. She and her husband live in Bethesda, Maryland. They are the parents of two grown sons and have three grandchildren: Sophia, Tressa, and Garrett.